THE STUDENT

The
Student

Cary
Fagan

Freehand Books acknowledges the financial support for its publishing program provided by the Canada Council for the Arts and the Alberta Media Fund, and by the Government of Canada through the Canada Book Fund.

 Canada Council for the Arts   Conseil des Arts du Canada   Alberta Government   Canada

Freehand Books
515 – 815 1st Street SW   Calgary, Alberta   T2P 1N3
www.freehand-books.com

Book orders: LitDistCo
8300 Lawson Road   Milton, Ontario   L9T 0A4
Telephone: 1–800–591–6250   Fax: 1–800–591–6251
orders@litdistco.ca   www.litdistco.ca

Library and Archives Canada Cataloguing in Publication
Title: The student / Cary Fagan.
Names: Fagan, Cary, author.
Identifiers: Canadiana (print) 20190047798
Canadiana (ebook) 20190047828
ISBN 9781988298443 (softcover)
ISBN 9781988298450 (html)
ISBN 9781988298467 (pdf)
Classification: LCC PS8561.A375 S78 2019 | DDC C813/.54—dc23

Edited by Deborah Willis
Book design by Natalie Olsen, Kisscut Design
Cover image © Aleksandra Jankovic / stocksy.com
Author photo by Mark Raynes Roberts
Printed on FSC® recycled paper and bound in Canada by Marquis

for

———————

REBECCA

———

1957

LATE SUMMER — AUTUMN

———

She walked dreamily along the curve of Queen's Park, the afternoon air heavy (not "brooding," she thought) and took notice of the broad leaves overhead, chestnut cases rattling. She pressed her books to her sweater, and stopped to look at the pigeon standing on the head of the equestrian statue, whose rider's name she could never remember. But surely it was a literally hollow symbol of adventurism, colonialism, the glory of war and all the rest.

Every year before the start of school some fraternity boys would set up a ladder in the dead of night and paint the horse's sex parts. Red this year. The paint would remain until the janitors came with their buckets and long-handled brushes. It was a shame they didn't have some political motivation, rather than acting like adolescents. Funny that she'd found it shocking the first year — blue was the colour then. And here she was about to start her final year, already nostalgic. How little she had known of anything back then!

As she walked on, a couple held hands as they passed the other way. The woman leaned in close to him and gave her a suspicious glance, the effect of which was to prompt her to re-evaluate how she had dressed that morning. Cashmere sweater over an ivory blouse, plain skirt and loafers with almost no heel. She wanted to be taken as a serious young woman, not a clothes horse. She was small and cute rather than pretty, with her long dark hair pulled back and dark eyes and perhaps too strong a chin that made her look like a small dog that wanted to bite somebody.

An older man's aromatic pipe smoke reached her pleasantly from his bench. None of her childhood friends smoked but a lot of the women at university did and of course she had tried but didn't see the point and, besides, they were always brushing their teeth like mad to get the stain off. A small pipe would be a statement, and everyone would chatter about it, only she wondered if it would be too mannish, like Gertrude Stein (was she holding a pipe in that Picasso portrait?). Perhaps it was even a signal of lesbianism, like going to a party in a man's suit, not that she'd actually seen anyone do it.

She crossed University Avenue and reached the sidewalk that sloped down to Hart House. And as she put her foot down the air sounded with ringing bells. It was the carillon in the tower, some music student pulling the chords or pressing the keys or however it worked, Bach it might have been although she couldn't be sure. It was easy for her to believe that the bells were ringing for her alone, were ringing a welcome for Miriam Moscowitz, honours English literature major with a minor in French. Of course, she thought, they *are* ringing for me!

She walked along the formidable stone front of Hart House. Most of the time the building was for men only, but when she mentioned it didn't seem fair, none of the other women she knew seemed to care a wit. As if they'd want to run around a track beside sweaty men or listen to ridiculous debates about whether Riel ought to have been hung or not! And hadn't they put in the new basement-level entrance so that a female accompanied by a man could have a cup of tea in the Arbor Room at certain hours?

As if they should be grateful for that! Yet she loved the university, as if she had found her true home. The lecture halls, the presentations and discussions in seminar rooms, the hours of library study. The sound of François Villon read aloud, or a late-night exposition of Donne's sacred and profane. Every year she had won a prize for one course or another, hiding her exultation behind a façade of modesty that surely everyone saw through. And this year was going to be the beginning, not the end. Ahead would be graduate school, and teaching and writing, a life of literature and thought if she did everything right, if she convinced those around her she deserved to be one of them.

She paused in the arch under the tower. As always, she made herself read a few of the inscribed names of the dead. As a child walking with her father during the war she had seen canvas tents pitched on the green circle. "You see them?" he had said, holding onto her hand. "They're going to risk their lives for us." She stared at the young men in their uniforms standing idly or sitting on canvas chairs, talking or playing cards or writing letters. Her father had gone up to a group, had spoken a few words and then shaken them by the hand, but when he was walking back to her she saw them chuckling. But that was so long ago. One of her professors had told them that they were on the cusp of history, the leading edge of the human story, but only a few students had understood the irony — for the present moment always is. She preferred to see his words as a deeper truth. That they really were living in a new time. There were too many bombs now for another war, which in any case would interfere with her future — and wasn't that as good as any reason for the shape of destiny?

The bells stopped ringing but their echo took seconds to fade away.

She walked briskly the few short steps to the east door of University College. It was her college and she thought of it in the most possessive terms. She'd heard that students at Victoria and St. Michael's looked down on those at U.C. as mongrels or infidels, and it was true that the Junior Common Room had been nicknamed the Jewish Common Room. But a person went to U.C. because he was intellectually ambitious, not a social climber. She loved the old Victorian building, grand yet peculiar and friendly. She pulled open the weighty door and slipped into the cool interior. She patted the exquisitely carved griffin on the newel post, which everyone mistakenly called a gargoyle, then walked down the hall, her heels tapping softly. Soon the place would be overrun with noisy returning students and diffident freshmen peering at the handmade signs for the camera club, politics club, winter ski trip, Spanish circle. But she had escaped her father's office and for now she had the building to herself and she exited into the arcade that surrounded the flagstone and grass quad that was enclosed by the college's three wings. Under the arcade were wooden doors where the professors had their dark little offices. To have one of those offices for your own, to plan your lectures, confer with your students, write your books! She might hide her ambition from her family and even from her friends, but she was clear in her own mind about what she felt capable of, and believed in, and wanted.

The sky was soft above the quad, ethereally clouded. She chose a bench, brushing it off with a tissue from her handbag, and placed the books down beside her. She had T.S. Eliot's essays and his *Four Quartets,* a small volume of Verlaine, *The Ambassadors,* and the first issue of the *Evergreen Review.* She'd gone to Britnell's for the James and then had seen the *Evergreen Review,* buying it for the story by Samuel Beckett. She would have liked to read it now but instead opened the essays because she was in the middle of one and always imposed on her studies a pleasurably strict discipline. Otherwise she might end up like the father in *To the Lighthouse,* whose thought (in that hilarious but terrifying moment) went from P to Q but could never get to R.

Last year Professor Reid had said that Virginia Woolf was of interest not as a writer but as a neurasthenic.

From her handbag she drew her compact mirror and lipstick for a quick touch-up, dropped them back in and took out her current notebook and a ballpoint. She began to read, tapping the end of the pen against her lip, wrote down a thought, read on, and was about to write again when a noise broke her concentration.

Not just a noise but a grunt. And then she heard it again, not a grunt but a snore.

Frowning, she forced her gaze to stay on the page. Next came muttering, the words not quite decipherable. She had to look up and there, across the small green square, was the culprit, someone sprawled on a bench with his own pile of books for a pillow. She sized him up — the wheat-coloured hair, narrow face, long legs in cotton trousers and worn shoes. His mouth twitched as from a dream or nightmare and then he turned away with a groan.

Why hadn't he found a sofa in the Hart House library, like the male students who were always going on about their naps? She found it impossible to go back to her reading. Instead, she stared at the back of his wrinkled jacket. She closed her book, not quite slamming it, gathered up the rest, and on a sudden impulse strode across the grass towards him. She would prod him between the shoulder blades with her pen and let him know what a nuisance he was.

He startled her by shifting onto his back. "Not... not now," he mumbled, and she quickly retreated several steps, then walked quickly away. Like a scared rabbit, she said to herself in disgust.

§

She was named Miriam after her great-grandmother on her father's side but, growing up, everyone called her Minnie. In her first days at university she had introduced herself as Miriam, and all her school friends called her so, although every time she met a childhood acquaintance on campus she feared getting tagged again. Living with her parents, she moved back and forth between the new world of Miriam and the old one of Minnie. The only benefit she could see was a particular sensitivity to the naming of characters in literature.

§

She almost always kept Isidore waiting. It was never her conscious intention to be late for their dates, although she couldn't deny knowing that it kept him in a state of anxiety and expectation. She was known for not giving a hoot about appearances, for saying that Madison Avenue and the whole fashion business were a conspiracy, and once she said to her oldest friend Faiga, "I'd be happy in a potato sack." Only after she said it did she remember having once seen a poor sharecropper's child wearing just such a sack and staring with large, resigned eyes into the lens of a *Life* magazine photographer.

In any case, it still took her considerable time to get ready. And on this night she chose her outfit carefully (a wool-crepe sheath dress) and then applied a thin black line around her eyes to make them look bigger and her nose smaller. A little powder to de-accentuate her stubborn chin.

Downstairs, Isidore was making awkward conversation with her father. Her father liked Isidore but she was sure that the very thought of him having some sort of intimate relation with his daughter filled his mouth with bile. Miriam didn't trip down the stairs as usual but descended with mock-dignity and Isidore, who had been strangling a fedora in his hands, turned to her with obvious relief. No doubt her father thought his hat brim too wide, like a hoodlum's.

"There you are, Minnie. We don't want to miss the start."

Her mother came in from the kitchen carrying a glass of ice water. Isidore thanked her and gulped half of it down. Her father, in his jacket and tie, held the evening edition of the *Star* under his arm. He also read the *Globe* in the morning, but not the *Telegram,* which he considered anti-Semitic. "And what are you going to see?" he asked, as if he kept up-to-date on the latest Hollywood movies when in fact he had no patience for them and refused to go with her mother even to *The Pajama Game.*

"A western," Isidore said. "Minnie indulges me. Thank you for the water. It really hit the spot."

Her mother took back the glass. "Mr. Moscowitz is a Coca-Cola drinker. He has three a day, don't you, dear? We should have bought stock in that company."

"I don't believe in stocks," her father said. "They're no different from gambling."

"Actually," Isidore said, "stockholders provide capital that help businesses to grow."

"You're disagreeing with my father?" said Miriam. "How brave of you."

"Well, I was only making a joke," her mother said. "My husband is too serious."

"You're not too serious, Daddy." Miriam, who saw the look of distress and knew well her power to change her father's mood in an instant, put a hand on his shoulder and kissed his cheek.

"It was nice to see you, Mr. and Mrs. Moscowitz," Isidore said. "My parents send their best. And say hi to Brian for me. I didn't see him."

"He's building a bridge from his chair to the bed," said her father. "He loves that Meccano set. I think maybe he'll be an engineer."

"I think it's more likely he'll blow bridges up," Miriam said lightly, putting on her camel-hair coat.

The Eglinton Theatre was only a couple of blocks away but Isidore insisted on driving, in case they wanted to go somewhere after, as if she didn't know what that meant. She thought of reminding him to call her Miriam but let it pass. They had started to go out at the end of high school, and even though she had thought it a mistake to get involved just as she was going to begin the life she wanted, she didn't stop herself. He was Jewishly handsome, black hair and eyebrows, a little full in the face, not tall but big-shouldered. Already he made a decent salary working for his father and he wore good suits, cut well for his figure, with a silk handkerchief in his pocket. They had even less in common now than when they had first gone out, but he let her talk, trying to understand what she was on about, and suddenly she would notice his pained expression, like a puppy confused by his master's command, and her heart went out to him even as she wanted to laugh out loud. Twice he had asked her to marry him, or rather talked about being married without quite asking, afraid of what she would say, so she hadn't felt obliged to give him an answer. But one day, she knew, he'd do something atrocious like get down on his knee. He was kind, and big-hearted, and devoted, and she told herself that she would marry him if she could get herself to say yes and wouldn't marry him if she couldn't, and that until the moment came she didn't have to decide.

So many people now stayed home to watch television, but she couldn't stand sitting in the living room staring at the fluttery screen. Her mother once told her about the Eglinton Theatre opening and how people had lined up to see a movie starring Jack Oakie, who nobody remembered anymore, but just as much to see the art deco furnishings. Miriam didn't know the name of the movie they were going to see until she glanced up at the marquee — *Gunfight at the O.K. Corral.* And really she didn't mind, not when she got to see Bergman and Akira Kurosawa at the university film society. And there was the French Cine Club at the Hyland Theatre where she went with three or four of her university friends every month. So she didn't mind seeing a Hollywood horse opera if it made Isidore happy.

And when the lights went up again, she found herself blinking and with only a fragmentary sense of the story, for her mind had drifted to her work, and the influence of certain new critics on her despite reservations, and the question of what the topic for her PhD thesis might be. After a movie Isidore was always hungry and they went into the Honey Dew where she had tea and he coffee with pie and ice cream. He wanted to talk about the film and so she went on about moral ambiguity until he interrupted her by saying, "Why are you trying to spoil the film? Come on, Minnie. Lancaster was the good guy and Douglas was the bad guy. All that studying is going to your head."

"Where else is it supposed to go to, my kidneys?"

He got that hurt look, which meant that she had made him feel dim. So she changed the subject by asking about the family dry cleaning business. "I tell you, we're coming on like gangbusters. It's all these suit-and-tie office jobs. And with all the new subdivisions there's only room to grow. We just signed a lease in Streetsville and we're thinking about getting into Don Mills. My father's still got me doing grunt-work, spending half my time driving from one store to the next, checking up on things. We had five workers call in sick yesterday from that Asian flu. I had to work the shirt-folder myself. But he'll see what I'm worth, the SOB. I'll be in head office by next year."

And then instead of driving the two blocks home, he suggested they go for a ride. They drove along Bloor and up Spadina while he fiddled with the radio, turning the knob from Elvis Presley, from Paul Anka, from Presley again to settle on Johnny Mathis singing "Chances Are." Along the high curve of Davenport they cruised, listening to the tinkling piano and quavering voice, turning through the old gate into the shadowy circle of Wychwood Park. Slowly they rolled past the pond to the old houses and long green lawns until he pulled up against the ditch and turned off the engine. They sat in the dark and she tried to turn towards him only she couldn't get herself to and just continued to stare through the curving windshield, feeling the vinyl beneath her dress. So he turned and leaned into her to kiss — his lips were always damp — and he slid his hand along the curve of her leg and up her dress and she found herself unpleasantly, or perhaps unwillingly, aroused, her breath catching, and she gently moved his hand away and put her own onto his bulge. She helped to open his trousers and he leaned back and closed his eyes. Was he gigantic compared to other men or were they all this big? With one hand always moving, she expertly opened the glove compartment to retrieve the box of tissue. He made almost comical noises, lurching forward so that she almost lost hold of him. And when he was done she balled up the tissues and snapped open her suede handbag and dropped them in.

He drove to Heddington. They kissed goodnight and he called, "Minnie—" but she was already closing the door with a wave and hurrying up the short flagstone path to the porch. She used her key, tiptoed upstairs to the bathroom where she flushed the tissues and washed her hands, looking at her small pale face in the mirror. She hiked up her dress to pee and washed her hands again and brushed her teeth. It wasn't so late that she couldn't read for at least a half hour before turning out the light.

§

Her father had relied on the same receptionist, Bessie Engelhardt, for almost seven years. He was a fastidious employer and Bessie, as Miriam's mother said, "fit him to a T." He had hired her out of Weller Secretarial School, where she had come first in shorthand, second in typing and bookkeeping. In fact, he had wondered why she hadn't preferred to work for an insurance firm or some larger company. Every morning she arrived ten minutes early, dressed modestly and with her hair clipped back. She called him Doctor Moscowitz although he was only a chiropodist, never booked appointments for difficult patients in the late afternoon, kept the billings up-to-date. When the city was struck by a series of holdups, she insisted on walking to the bank with him. Her father knew nothing of Bessie's family or private life aside from the fact that she lived with her mother in Etobicoke. When she told him that she had flat feet, he insisted that she be treated by someone else.

Miriam made quick judgments about people. She imagined Bessie going home after work to make dinner with her mother and then listening to the radio until it was time for bed. She rather inappropriately laughed when her father came home from work and told them that Bessie was pregnant. He was so shaken that he had to sit at the kitchen table and drink a glass of water before recounting how Bessie had waited for him in the office that morning. She had burst into tears, throwing her arms around him.

Her father, Miriam knew, was susceptible to a woman in distress. He often visited her mother's younger sister, who suffered from depression and sometimes wouldn't leave her house or cook for her children. He saved their neighbour Mrs. Klotz, by killing a bat in her kitchen with a tennis racquet. But her father had his limits. Miriam easily imagined him disentangling himself from Bessie's sobbing embrace and then removing his own glasses to methodically wipe them with a small cloth, his habit when he needed a moment. He had sat her down in the reception room and after asking a series of delicate questions had paced about the room, eying his watch for the arrival of the first patient. She could stay with her sister in Sault

Ste. Marie until the baby was born, he said, telling people there that her husband was in Korea. When the baby was born, Jewish Family Services would find it a home. She would suffer distress and possibly sadness but a few weeks should bring her back to her usual efficient self, when she could renew her regular life as if nothing had happened. Of course she couldn't return to her present position, but he would write a sincere letter of recommendation.

"Are you sure it wasn't you who tempted her?" Miriam's mother said, probably annoyed by the embrace.

"That is a revolting thing to say. And in front of Minnie."

"I'm surprised you let me hear any of it," Miriam said. "And I don't even understand. What exactly did Bessie *do?*"

Her father did not find this funny. He found a way to change her mood — by suggesting that she become his receptionist for the summer. Miriam needed a job anyway and there was no reason to work for a stranger.

"No, please, don't ask me to," she pleaded. "I'll find something else. I can't work in your office all day."

"It's a very good idea," her mother said. "And you can be agreeable for once in your life."

"Minnie has to spend the summer smelling people's feet!" said Brian, who was nine years younger and who she had as little to do with as possible.

"Oh, shut up."

"There's no need for that kind of language," her father said. "It'll be very nice having my own daughter around."

"Don't be surprised if I start every day by vomiting in the sink," she said and took herself upstairs.

§

Her father's office was on the second floor of a yellow building on College Street. On the first floor was a delicatessen and a religious store selling mezuzot and tefillin. In the next office was an employment agency and on the floor above a small leather factory where women sat at machines making gloves. Further down Spadina were the Tower, the Balfour, and other loft buildings, and while some of the factories had closed, the workers in these buildings were still the source of most of her father's customers. They spoke a shrugging, skeptical Yiddish to one another but English to her father because he was the "doctor."

Miriam's place was behind the waiting room desk, next to the wall clock and the calendar from the Jewish Burial Society. The chair had scraped shallow troughs into the linoleum floor. On the desk sat a telephone, a card file, and a hardbound appointment book. Along the wall were oak filing cabinets, bought second-hand, filled with patients' folders. One door led to the examination room and another to a small washroom where her father retreated after each patient to vigorously scrub his hands and also gargle, for he was conscious of his breath.

Behind the desk chair was a hook from which Miriam would take the white smock and horrid little nurse's cap, the same that Bessie Engelhardt had worn. She placed files in order on the corner of the desk for her father to pick up. She answered the phone and wrote appointments into the book. After the departure of each patient she had to enter the examination room with a spray bottle of disinfectant and a paper towel.

To patients her father spoke in a reassuring voice. He dealt with a succession of clawtoes, hammertoes, in-grown nails, bunions, corns, deformities, infections. Occasionally he would call her in for assistance — to help raise an elderly patient or unwrap a bandage — and she would feel herself gagging. During the half-hour lunch break she could hardly eat. Instead, she would hurry over to Bellevue Park and sit among the elderly Jewish and Italian women while reading a volume of Auden, which she believed absolutely necessary for saving her life.

Sometimes she didn't come home for dinner but met Isidore at a restaurant or for dancing. Isidore was a good dancer, having taken lessons as a teenager. One night they went to see the Jimmy Coxson Orchestra. Her feet hurt in a new pair of heels and as soon as he dropped her off at home she pulled them off. She crept upstairs to find on her pillow a small hardcover book. Dr. Marion Hilliard, *A Woman Doctor Looks at Love and Life.* Evidently it had been left by her mother, who had been alarmed by the

Bessie Engelhardt affair. Over the years her mother had left a series of pamphlets on being a girl and then a teenager, each of which she had read with giddy horror. Now she sat on the edge of the bed and opened the book. The author was chief of obstetrics and gynecology at Women's College Hospital in Toronto. Of course she was impossible to embarrass now and the book was sure to be a lark, so she opened it at random.

Any doctor can chart the progress of love-making in marriage — a strained honeymoon, a span of approximately five years before sexual adjustment is perfect, a crisis after ten years because both partners are full of yearnings and misery, another crisis after twenty-five years because of an overwhelming sense of bleakness.

Thank you, Dr. Hilliard, she thought, closing it again. She let herself fall backwards onto the bed. Perhaps one ought to get engaged, buy the dress, cut the cake, dance oneself silly, and then blow one's brains out with a gun.

§

She was freed from the confines of her father's office by the annual family holiday. Each year they rented a cottage on the south shore of Lake Simcoe, in the section where Jews could buy property, the drives marked by wooden signs:

The Horvaths, The Targovetskys, Camp Kugel. On Friday
night candles could be seen burning in cottage windows.

When she was younger, Miriam overcame her fear of
diving by kneeling on the dock and falling headfirst into
the water, then getting out, rising a few inches higher, and
falling again. After Brian was born and with her mother
occupied most of the time, she began to run with a pack
of kids, playing tag between the cottages, taking over the
public volleyball court, learning Israeli folk dances from
a young woman who had spent a summer on a Kibbutz. At
fifteen she began to spend more of her time alone, reading
in a Muskoka chair or suntanning on the dock. Now it was
Brian who threw himself into the cold lake, or pretended
to bushwack in his Davy Crockett cap.

A new receptionist started in time for Miriam to drive
Brian and her mother up in the family car. Her father came
by bus on the two Friday afternoons, holding in his lap their
pastrami order from Switzer's and a twisted challah. As
he trudged up the drive the family greeted him like a con-
quering hero, rushing to relieve him of his burdens. She and
Brian would unpack the groceries while their parents took
a few steps together. It was the only time she saw them hold
hands. When they returned, her father praised the quality of
the air as if he hadn't said the same thing last year. He would
roll up his trousers and sleeves. Brian went to the ice box to
fetch him a Coca-Cola. Most of the mosquitoes were gone
and she and her mother would set the picnic table for dinner.

This year she had asked to stay home by herself; she was too old to vacation with her family. Her parents acted incredulous. What else should children do until they were married? Didn't Faiga Lasky go to Miami Beach at Christmas with her parents? And *she* was married.

It wasn't so hard to give in and spend a couple of weeks in halter tops and shorts, a floppy hat and cat's eyes sunglasses. She dragged the chair onto the dock and sat for hours with her pile of books and her notebook. When her mother brought out a glass of lemonade, Miriam held out her hand without looking up.

"Don't forget," said her mother, who was evidently still standing just behind her. "Andrei is coming tomorrow and you'll have to pick him up."

"I know, I know." And why did her father have to invite Andrei? For four days, and during the week when her father wasn't even here? It was a conspiracy to deprive her of solitude.

She underlined a passage in Brooks and Warren's *Understanding Poetry*. As the sun began to lower she removed her hat and shook out her hair. When she needed a break she picked up a paperback copy of *Maigret à l'école* to help improve her comprehension. And all the while she let the idea for a thesis float in her mind, something to do with the French poets and their influence on early T.S. Eliot.

"Hi there!" someone shouted at her. She tipped up her sunglasses to see three bare-chested young men in a canoe.

"What's your name?" another one called.

"Sorry, I'm reading."

"There's a dance at the lodge tonight. Want to go?"

She waved them off without looking up.

A paddle dipped noisily and one of them muttered, "Stuck-up Jewish bitch," making the others laugh. She flinched and pretended to keep reading.

§

Her family had known Andrei Unterman for five years, seven if she counted the letters he wrote before his disembarkation in Halifax. Back in the letter days, Miriam used to refer to him as the "sad case" — as in, "Have we received another missive from the sad case?" Her father used to get very angry and, really, how could she have made fun of a young man who had lost his parents, his sisters, his brother, his grandparents, his aunts and uncles? Because his written English wasn't perfect?

Reading those letters aloud at the supper table, her father would leave out parts that he considered too disturbing and she would have to go hunting for them afterwards. When the war was over and he had recovered some of his strength he'd been permitted to go to school in Zurich, and from there had been accepted at the University of Toronto on the condition that he find a sponsor. Jewish Immigrant Aid Services had contacted her father. His heartfelt desire, Andrei Unterman wrote to the Moscowitz family, was to become a lawyer and work within the strictures of the great British legal system which would never have allowed such atrocities. Her father agreed to insure that he did not become a burden on Canadian society.

Three days after his arrival he came to the house for Friday dinner. Her father recited the brucha over the bread and wine but Andrei did not say as much as an *Amen*. When asked a question he would think an uncomfortably long time before answering. His most frequent expression was thank you: thank you for the invitation, for being asked to sit down, for being offered the brisket, for water. He didn't eat much. Her mother served apple strudel for dessert and as he looked at his piece he began to weep, his narrow shoulders trembling.

Andrei had already found a place to live, a boarding house on Markham Street. He was soon working at two part-time jobs, in a shoemaking factory near the waterfront and delivering parcels by wobbly bicycle. He came every Friday night but after two years of undergraduate study and three in law school, he still looked undernourished.

It was hardly surprising that he adored them. He nodded gravely at her father's pronouncements, leapt up to help her mother carry a dish, and after dinner he sat patiently with Brian, examining the latest entries in his scrapbook dedicated to the space program. For a long time he seemed unsure about Miriam, possibly because she wasn't as nice as the others. "Of course he's in love with me," Miriam told Faiga. "I'm the first girl he met here." Over time he grew easier around her and learned to make mild jokes at her expense, or offer some remark to deliberately rile her up. She would start to rant and then the trick would dawn on her and she would laugh.

§

The cottage bedroom had plywood walls and a small window. It was too hot in the afternoon and began to smell of tar. Miriam stripped off her bathing suit and threw on a sundress and spent a minute at the bathroom mirror. In the kitchen her mother was trying to get the oven lit. "I told that thief Klonsky to get it fixed. He won't put in a penny."

"It's already a furnace in here. You're not going to heat the place up even more?"

"At six o'clock you'll want your dinner, won't you?"

"All right, Ma, I'm late. Where are the keys?"

"On the table. Take your brother."

"As if I could find him."

They sounded like a mother and daughter in some radio comedy. She pushed open the flimsy door and walked to the Chevrolet, got in and backed up the narrow path, then breezed along the gravel road, past the Targovetsky kid leaning a fishing rod on his shoulder like some Jewish Huck Finn. On the asphalt road she sped towards Barrie, her arm dangling out the open window. Soon she was rolling past the movie theatre and the hair salon and the shop selling inflatable rings. She slowed as the bus station came into view and there on the sidewalk was Andrei, sweating in his only suit, a small suitcase bound with twine at his feet. He looked worried, as if sure that he'd been forgotten, and when she honked he practically jumped out of his skin. He picked up his suitcase and hopped to the car, placing it carefully in the back seat before getting in beside her.

"Thank you for picking me up, Miriam."

He never called her Minnie. "If I didn't you'd probably end up wandering in the woods."

"Well, I brought a compass just in case."

"Really?"

"Yes, it points to 'Lost,' 'Very Lost,' and 'Give Up all Hope.'"

"Ha. Anyway, it isn't exactly wilderness here. Every afternoon there's a traffic jam on the lake."

"I suspect you're exaggerating. And look, I see quite a lot of trees. When I was little we once went to a resort on the Baltic Sea. The sand was nice. My parents looked almost relaxed. We ate fish every night."

And what was she supposed to say? That she was sorry his family was dead and she hoped that being here didn't depress the hell of him even though it ought to? For once she kept her mouth shut.

"Your father was very kind to ask me. I tried to refuse but he wouldn't let me. But I know you are studying and I promise to stay out of your way. I will be like a mouse."

"We've already got plenty of mice in the cottage. I'm sure you can use a break from your three jobs."

"Only two."

"I thought you were ambitious."

"You have — what's the expression? You have the wrong guy."

It sounded even funnier than he intended. "Don't worry, I'm very good at ignoring people. I've got a talent for it."

"Now you are making the joke."

"No, I'm serious. You'll see."

"Okay-doke."

He started to whistle. She said nothing for a full minute. "Fine. Am I supposed to recognize that tune?"

"'Love Letters in the Sand.'"

"Pat Boone? Please. And that's not even how it goes."

They pulled up the gravel drive to the cottage. Her mother came through the door, wiping her hands on her apron. Andrei got out and gave her a hug that knocked her half off balance. Brian appeared running from around back and urged Andrei to come swim. Miriam wondered if Brian saw Andrei as the brother he wished he had instead of her as a sister.

"I brought something for you," Andrei told Brian. "But later, when you don't have anything better to do."

It turned out that he didn't own a bathing suit. Her mother fetched one of her father's, a red-and-black diamond pattern, and as he came out of the bedroom he was to share with Brian he pulled the drawstring as tight as it would go. He was hollow-chested and white as an onion.

"You come in, too, Minnie."

She was surprised enough at her brother's request to agree. By the time she had changed into a one-piece suit, Brian was already in the water, taunting Andrei to follow. He stood with his hands wrapped around himself; perhaps he didn't know how to swim. And then suddenly he sprinted off the dock, howling like Johnny Weissmuller. Brian hooted his approval.

"Now you, Minnie!"

Her own dive was clean as a knife. The water was a cold shock that stunned her for a moment and then felt wonderful.

Andrei proved himself to be good company, careful not to intrude on her thoughts yet always ready to talk when she wanted. They got in the habit of going for a short walk after every meal, down to the boat launch and back. He didn't flirt or stare wistfully and she was relieved if also a little disappointed that his crush had faded.

The evenings he devoted to Brian, who was currently obsessed with the Russian dog that was about to go into space. He had a grainy photograph of Laika, cut from the newspaper, in the scrapbook he had insisted on bringing to the cottage, and he used it to draw his own pictures of the small, alert-looking dog ears that stood up, their tips flopped forward. Andrei lay on the rag rug with him, helping to colour in the pictures. Did Laika understand what was happening? What had his training been like? Was he scared? Miriam sat in a chair by the window listening. Her brother sounded excited but also anxious, as if he'd never worried about anything as much.

"Laika is going to be a hero," Andrei said. "And when he's back they will hold a parade in Red Square."

"For a dog?" Brian laughed, but he immediately began to draw a picture of a parade. His perspective was quite good. A short time later Andrei gave the boy his present, a Mr. Potato Head kit. Miriam thought he was too old for it, but Brian was thrilled. He abandoned his drawing and spent the rest of his time until bed sticking the plastic parts into a potato and making them all admire what he had made.

The time moved slowly and then suddenly it was gone. They all got in the car to drive Andrei into Barrie. On the ride he thanked them over and over. At the bus station he pulled out his sad little suitcase, turned to wave and walked away.

§

Now fall classes began with an invasion of students. They streamed into the chemistry and mining buildings, stood smoking on the steps of convocation hall, lugged suitcases and portable typewriters and guitars into the residences. The young men wore V-neck sweaters or blazers and ties, the women were in blouses and turtlenecks, corduroy and tartan skirts. A rugger team practised on the field, watched by two young ministers in the doorway of Knox College. A quartet singing "Swanee River" was largely ignored. Miriam felt pleasantly superior to the freshmen, who stared like lost puppies or walked with a tower of new books in their arms.

Her English classes were held in the same second-floor room of University College, and the others were tucked into various buildings nearby. On Monday she had "New Critical Approaches to Modern Poetry," for which she had been reading all summer. The professor was new, a young, pockmarked man born in the prairies but with a degree from Oxford. Tuesday was *fin de siècle* French literature with the same instructor as last year, who had spent his summer in Switzerland and gave them a slide show. Political Science was the same afternoon and Wednesday was Greek art and its influence on the Renaissance.

On Friday she returned to the second-floor room in U.C. for Professor Birmingham's Jacobean Drama. She knew the younger instructors dismissed Birmingham as old-fashioned, but she loved his Shakespeare and Romantic poetry courses. He was at least seventy, very tall with a long, dirty-coloured beard and a thick Scottish brogue. "What can there be after Shakespeare but a terrible decline?" he said, leaning on the edge of his desk. "Love, beauty, nobility, not to mention genius — chuck all of those notions out the window. Instead we are left with scoundrels and fools and hypocrites, with stupidity, selfishness, deviancy, and an ugly moral relativism reflecting the politics of the age of James the First. But if our playwrights have not produced many immortal works, they did make thrilling theatre for their age. And even to our modern sensibilities they can be jolly good, offensive fun. I warn you that this is bloody stuff, ladies and gentlemen, and not for the faint of heart."

Professor Birmingham let his eyes rest on her in the front row. He gave her a slight smile and continued on. From her first visit to his office three years ago they had developed an easy rapport. He had leant her books and told her about famous productions he had seen. They argued often, for he disapproved of her "hermetic" readings of a text, but he had never given a paper of hers less than an A. Once last year he had introduced her to the dean as "my best, my most challenging, and my most aggravating student." She knew that he was an ever-grieving widower, that his children lived in England and Australia, that he would be perfectly happy to "keel over" before finishing his book on *Hamlet*. All of this he had told her, ignoring her polite noises about how busy he must be as she tried to edge to the door. Sometimes he offered her a flask of good Scottish whiskey that he kept in a drawer.

And now all her plans depended on him. He was highly respected, well-connected and had a place on several important committees, including one that gave out monetary prizes for graduate school. A good word from him would go far. She needed his recommendation. If only she could get up the courage to ask.

§

On Friday evening a light rain. The shops were closed but the restaurant windows glowed through their curtains. Miriam slouched along with her friends, up from the dark campus to the street lights on Bloor. Beside her walked Nathan Gorman, who had finally won the editorship of the *Gargoyle* and bounced, Miriam thought, with gleeful self-importance. Deborah Kersh, her closest university friend, was almost as short as her but with a pleasant round face that made most males stupidly uninterested in her. Behind them came Irving Sharpe, Judith Tanz and Michael Singer, and now Deborah was explaining why she was looking to escape Whitney for a shared apartment. "Nobody agrees on anything. If you touch another girl's hairbrush you risk starting World War Three. The bathrooms smell. There isn't enough hot water in the shower and the drains are full of hair."

"And here I was imagining a harem," Michael said. "You're shattering my illusions."

"It'll do you good," Judith said. She and Michael had been going out since last spring and now he put his hand proprietarily on her ass. Judith often discussed her sex life with Miriam and Deborah, although Deborah was acknowledged as the more knowledgeable as she had slept with her Spanish graduate instructor.

"There is something," Deborah said, "that unites everyone in the residence."

"Menstruation?" ventured Irving.

Deborah swatted him. "Hatred for our house mother. She's a real bitch —"

They dodged a station wagon and crossed over to the Blue Cellar Room. Half the tables were already occupied by other students and Nathan felt obliged to stop at several of them and exchange aggressive witticisms. He pointedly ignored a group of Victoria College Literary Society members. The friends took over their own round table and without looking at the menu ordered several platters to share and two carafes. The wine, as usual, arrived immediately.

"So what are you going to say about the play?" Michael asked Nathan.

"Good question. The important thing is that I appear smarter than the reader, if not the playwright. I suppose I'll start with some smartass remark about Sartre."

"I can't say I liked it," said Judith. "The whole thing was ridiculous."

"It's *supposed* to be," Nathan said. "It's *absurd*. And I get the existentialism, but when he threw in that stuff about the war he really confused me. Undermined my confidence in my own shiny opinion."

"The acting was stiff," Irving said. "And that one woman, the one who cheated on her older husband, she wasn't cast right. She should have been much better-looking."

"Now *that's* ridiculous," Judith said.

"I agree," said Miriam. "About it being ridiculous, I mean."

"The play had an ugly view of people," Deborah said. "That is, if you take its portraits seriously. They're drawn pretty broadly, especially their moral failings."

"I didn't feel any emotional response, if that means anything," Irving said. "But then you all tell me I have no feelings. But maybe it was the translation. Have you read the original, Miriam?"

Miriam had her wine glass. She liked that they deferred to her in matters of French. "I read it last year. The title doesn't really mean 'no exit.' It's more like 'behind closed doors' or maybe 'closed session.' Watching it actually performed, I wondered about its influence on Beckett. You might say that the characters in *Waiting for Godot* are stuck in a similar kind of hell. The difference,

I think, is that the Sartre's is an idea dramatized — his characters talk about suffering. Beckett's characters — we actually feel them suffering."

"Maybe you want to do the review," Nathan said. "I need more writers anyway."

"Miriam," Deborah raised her eyebrows, "is not a mere journalist."

They laughed but it was true. She liked the idea of writing for the paper but worried that it was too easy. She wanted to write criticism that itself aspired to the level of art, or something close to it.

"The only reason I write for your rag is so I can have access to the office," Irving said. "I take my best naps on that sofa. Plus Nathan keeps a box of animal crackers on his desk."

The waitress slid the platters onto the table. None of them would eat pork except Michael, who gleefully piled the chops onto his plate.

Irving said, "Sartre found a wife *and* a mistress, and he looks like a little troll. Of course she —"

"Don't," Miriam interjected. "Just don't say anything nasty about Simone de Beauvoir. Or you'll get my mashed potatoes on your head."

Irving held up his hands in surrender.

"We need more wine," Nathan said.

§

Sometimes she thought there was something genuinely wrong with Brian. For one thing, he didn't have any friends. At least, he never had another boy over or got asked to somebody's house. And her parents, who liked having him around at every moment, didn't seem to notice. But then it wasn't as if they had many friends, either. Her mother saw only her sister, and when her father wasn't working he just wanted to be home. She sometimes thought that there was an unhealthy anti-social streak in her family, one that she had only partly managed to suppress.

Most of the time Brian was just a pest, but every so often she looked at him and felt a pang of concern and, possibly, remorse. And here he was on the front porch, his back half sticking out of the big cardboard box from her mother's new electric range. He had crayoned *Sputnik 2* on the side in odd-looking letters that must have been intended to mimic the Cyrillic alphabet. He was holding a biscuit in his hand just beyond the opening and trying to induce the neighbourhood dog into the box with him. "Come on, come on, Roscoe," he kept saying. "Get the nice treat, come on." The excited dog kept moving towards him, making little yips, and then backing away again.

She had to step over the dog to get into the house. "Ah, you've scared him off," Brian complained.

"A good thing. He'll probably give you fleas." She went into the house, calling, "Ma!" as she took off her coat.

Miriam found her in the kitchen. "You're early for a change," her mother said. She had cut out the dough for verenekas and was pinching them closed around the stuffing.

"Actually, I can't stay. I just came home to change my clothes."

Her mother's hands stopped but she didn't look at her daughter, which Miriam knew was a bad sign. "Twice already this week you haven't been home for dinner."

"I know, I know. But I have to go back to school. There's a meeting. We're trying to get the funds to bring Pete Seeger in to perform."

"That's a Jewish name?"

"He's a communist," said Brian, coming into the kitchen. "He gets arrested all the time."

"You shouldn't be mixed up in it," her mother said. "Your father wouldn't approve. Just ask him when he comes home."

"It's important to be involved, Ma. That's part of what school is about. And he isn't a communist, I don't think." She came up behind her mother and leaned over to kiss her cheek.

"Tomorrow is Friday. Andrei is coming. You have to be here."

"Aren't I always here Fridays? Anyway, Andrei comes every week."

She ran upstairs to take a quick shower and then put on a clean skirt and blouse. She put on lipstick and ran down the stairs, calling out her goodbye. She reached the corner of Bathurst and Eglinton just as the bus was pulling up and she waved for the driver to wait as she crossed over. But on the bus ride down she felt less and less inclined to go to the meeting, which was bound to drag on endlessly. People always thought what they had to say was so important. Instead, she decided to go to the library. She much preferred to study.

§

At midmorning the flagstones under her feet looked the colour of Payne's grey. It was a colour named after the eighteenth-century painter — to know a fact like that was a protection and a comfort. She stood under the arches in the quad, listening to the sound of birds. The door she stood before belonged to Professor Birmingham, who'd awarded her a prize last year for her essay on Coleridge's "This Lime-Tree Bower My Prison," about which she had written everything she could think of except the simple truth that it was the most beautiful poem she had ever read.

Knock with determination, she told herself.

Throat clearing from inside. "Yes, yes, come."

The room was dark as a cave, the lead-paned windows half-blocked by towers of books. A desk lamp cast its green circle. Professor Birmingham was tamping tobacco into his pipe. "Miss Moscowitz, I'm very glad to see you. Let me just give my attention to getting this thing to draw properly. It was a gift from my brother in South Africa and it's made out of some damnable exotic wood."

She stood there as he fiddled with it, lighting a wooden match and cupping the flame over the bowl. The walls were lined with books and more were heaped on the threadbare rug. If this were her study she would remove the dirty curtains from the small window, paint the shelves, bring light and order.

At last curls of smoke appeared; they seemed to be coming out of his ears. "I think that's it. Sit, my dear, we don't stand on ceremony. How are you finding the Jacobeans? Sensational enough for you?"

"I can hardly imagine them being on the stage."

"Once in a while the RSC will do one. Trust me, it's a delicious orgy of blood."

"I wanted to do a little extra reading, actually. I've made up a supplemental list and I was hoping you might glance at it."

"Well, well, give it here," he said, extending a mottled hand. His fingernails were long and discoloured. "Yes, these lesser plays of Chapman and Heywood are worth reading. I wouldn't bother with John Ford unless you like peering into a truly unhealthy mind. And James Shirley, good, he's the last. How about some additional Middleton?

I wouldn't bother with Marston unless you really want to be thorough. And some parallel historical texts? I'll jot a couple down. Have you got any studies?"

"Just Wells."

"Nothing of Ellis-Fermor? This should keep you busy enough."

"Thank you, I appreciate it."

"Whatever else am I here for? Very glad to do it. And here's this pipe gone out again."

He capped his pen and handed back the paper. She wanted to make her getaway now but didn't see how speaking to him would be easier any other time so she tried to find her courage.

"I do have one more favour to ask, Professor."

"How can I be of service?"

"I'm hoping that you'll write a letter of reference for me."

"The heart and mind are both willing, my dear. Do you have employment in mind? Or is it teacher's college?"

"Actually it's here. I'm going to apply to the graduate department."

He avoided looking at her but took the pipe from his mouth. "Whatever for?"

The question took her aback. "Well, to do my Masters and then my PhD."

"No, no, I mean whatever do you want to do a PhD for? To spend several years of your life, not to mention the valuable resources of this university, for nothing? You'll get married and that will be the end of it. And a spot that could have gone to a genuinely worthy candidate will have been wasted."

"But it won't be. It's what I care about. It's what I want to do. To write, I mean, and to teach."

He pressed his fingers to his forehead. "So you say, but what I've seen all these years tells me differently. Besides, you'll never get a position. As I say, it's a waste."

"I don't see why I won't get a position. My marks —"

"As if that's the point. Miss Moscowitz, look at this very university. You certainly can't expect to be hired by any of the other colleges. That leaves only this one. And there has never been a female professor here. The hiring committee — well, trust me, I know them all well. And they are not about to change that."

"Aren't you on the committee?"

"You must understand. We are trying to maintain a first-rate department. We have to live up to the standards, of McGill, of Princeton and Harvard, of Oxford. Otherwise how are we to attract the best men out of the undergraduate departments? I'm sure you can put aside your own self-interest for a moment and understand the greater good. Now this has been a very unpleasant conversation and I am not pleased to have been forced into it. Good day, Miss Moscowitz."

She felt herself welling up. I will not cry, she told herself, I will not. She sniffed just once and managed to look straight at him. "Yes, thank you, good day," she said, standing up too quickly. She felt dizzy a moment and clasped the arm of the chair. Then she pushed it back and got around it, careful not to knock over any books on her way out.

§

She didn't go to her afternoon class, the first time in four years that she had missed a session when she wasn't ill. She buttoned her coat to the top, for it was grey and cold, and fished a pair of calfskin gloves from her pocket. What she felt most was a terrible embarrassment or shame that made her cheeks burn. It felt as if she had done something very wrong, something that would make everyone she knew feel disappointed in her. Also a physical churning in her stomach so that she suddenly needed a toilet and panicked that she would have an actual accident.

Luckily there was a restaurant at the corner. She called for a coffee as she passed the counter for the wash-room. It smelled of urine and she thought that she might throw up but she got onto the toilet and covered her eyes with her hands and hoped that nobody could hear.

Her face washed and clothes straightened, she went out again and put down some change for the coffee waiting on the counter but didn't stop. When a man standing at the corner looked at her, she stared back hard until he looked away and it made her feel a little triumph. She thought of all the things that had comforted her in her life. When she was a child and had a stuffed bear, pathetically small, but she had slept with it for years. And after that had been a pair of patent-leather shoes that she would put on in her room and pretend to be a princess, a famous dancer, or — absurdly — a woman aviator. But after that it was pretty classics in a row on her shelf, *Little Women* and *The Secret Garden* and *Anne of Green Gables*, books about children whose lives she wished were her own. And since then it had always been books, only she could not bear or deserve to open one now.

She was not even making sense to herself.

In front of her was a painting in a window. *The Park Gallery*, the sign said. She stepped inside and, pretending to be a regular person, walked around and looked at the paintings on the walls. They were all abstracts, the kind of work she had only seen reproduced in magazines. It was a group show and there was a lot of variation, thin or thick paint, wiggly brush strokes, straight lines made with a scraper of some sort. This one with the purple blotch was aggressive, that one with the fine line arcing over a red background was delicate. Some were plain ugly.

There was nobody else in the gallery but for a man behind a desk, and when he looked up at her she left the gallery.

She usually avoided the rush hour and was almost surprised to see the subway and then the bus so crowded with people heading home from work. If she got a job as a teacher, maybe in high school, she would be one of them. She had gone to North Toronto Collegiate and had known a couple of inspiring teachers there, especially for grade thirteen English, Mr. Hale. He had led her to Thomas Wolfe and D.H. Lawrence, E.M. Forster and Somerset Maugham. Surely that was a valuable life and if she got married she could leave work and then perhaps return a few years later, when her own children were in school. Not that she felt any strong desire for children, or thought for one minute about having a family the way her friend Faiga always had. Mr. Hale had been a good teacher, but their talks were at best expressions of enthusiasm and near the end of the year he had started to make her feel uncomfortable in a way that she found impossible to tell anyone about. It was how he leaned over her to look at her notebook and his suggestion that they meet for coffee after class, so that in the end she had pretended to join the swim club with practices every day after school.

The bus pulled up to Eglinton. She joined the line filing out into the softer light before evening. She had been talking to herself like a madwoman all the way home and she talked on, walking past the shops, and turned onto Heddington. As she passed each front door she placed her verdict on the people within: Mr. Corngold, braggart; the Metcalfes, colourless; Mrs. Zeligman, a malicious gossip. Up ahead some kids were running around. The street was often used for stickball and games of tag. She herself had spent obsessive hours skipping with her friends, and it had been frighteningly competitive. But today they were all boys, and although they were too far up the street to see them properly she could easily identify Brian by his short red jacket. He didn't usually join in, so that was something.

But something was off. She drew closer and saw there was a boy in the middle, the others running around him. Running and darting towards the boy and shouting. She hurried her pace, passing her own house and straining to hear better. The boy in the middle was crying. He was crying but he was also angry, or was trying to appear so as he fended off the circling boys. He was a little taller than any of them, with a shock of pale hair and trousers that were too short.

"*Swine! Dirty, dirty swine!*" one of the boys yelled.

She stopped when she saw Brian scoop something from the ground, a stone perhaps. He threw it as he ran. It hit the boy but he didn't react, only kept his eyes on the moving circle, sometimes turning around himself, keeping his hands in front.

"*Dirty German! Nazi! Go back where you came from! Go to hell!*"

She had to stop these boys from tormenting the one in the middle, but she felt her own fear as she watched. Before she could get herself to move somebody rushed past her from behind. She saw Andrei Unterman's hopping gait, his second-hand overcoat flapping around him. He paused a moment and then stepped into the circle, holding up his hands to stop them from crashing into him.

"What are you doing? This is shocking behaviour! If your parents saw you, what would they think? Go home, all of you, right now. You too, Brian. Go home."

The boys themselves stood and looked at him, as if undecided as to how seriously to take the thin man with his awkwardly waving hands. Then one of them bolted and the rest too broke away, heading for their own front doors. Some ran past her, including Brian, who seemed not to see her. A moment later there was only Andrei leaning down, his hand on the strange boy's shoulder.

"*Ich hasse sie,*" gasped the boy between sobs.

"*Sie kennen nichts besseres.*" Andrei spoke quietly. "*Wie heisst du?*"

The boy wiped his nose on his sleeve. He didn't look at Andrei but down the street, as if making sure they didn't come back. Andrei fished a handkerchief from his pocket.

She turned around and walked to her own house.

§

She went to bed early and slept in, coming down pale and bleary in her robe. Her father was already at work, while Brian was running outside the front window, yesterday seemingly forgotten, a feather stuck in a band around his head and a homemade bow in his hand. Why did every Jewish boy want to be a cowboy, or better yet, an Indian?

She walked into the kitchen to see her mother putting a bundt pan into the oven. On the counter was a plate of finger sandwiches.

"You cutting off crusts?" Miriam said, pushing a sandwich into her mouth. "I thought it was a waste."

"Those aren't for you." Her mother pulled the plate away. Only now did Miriam notice that her apron was tied over a chiffon dress.

"So who's coming over?"

"People."

"It's a secret?"

"As if I have secrets. Three women from the PTA. We have to plan a fundraiser for gymnasium equipment. As if I care about gymnasium equipment. But they asked me to join, and they're all friends with each other, and I don't know why I said yes."

"It'll be good for you, Ma."

"It'll be terrible. I have a headache already." She looked as if she might cry but still she trimmed more sandwiches. "There's something wrong with me."

Nothing made Miriam feel worse than seeing her mother in distress. She slipped her arms around her waist and leaned her cheek against her broad back. "There's nothing wrong with you, Ma."

"And I've gained weight. I could hardly zip up this dress. I'm surprised your father still looks at me."

"You shouldn't care about those old biddies."

"You can help me set the table." Her mother pulled away. "Then you better get ready."

"Ready for what? I'm not going to do a thing today." Miriam went over to the stove and put her hand on the side of the percolator to see if the coffee was still warm.

"For Isidore. He telephoned a while ago to see if you were up yet. He's coming to get you."

She rolled her eyes. "We don't have a date. It's not even noon. I don't want to go anywhere."

"I wouldn't want to be your boyfriend. Go and make yourself nice."

She went upstairs with a cup of lukewarm coffee and drank it in the bathroom as she put on a shower cap and turned on the hot water. Afterwards she dressed in an old shirt and a pair of slacks and when she reached the top of the stairs she saw Isidore in the front hall below. He held a bunch of roses, an unreal red, wrapped in newspaper.

"Is it my birthday?" She came down and kissed his cheek. "Mom? Apparently I'm going out. Can you put these flowers in a vase for me?"

Not waiting for an answer, she left them on the hall table and grabbed her coat. Isidore took her arm and opened the passenger door of his car for her. He pulled the car away smoothly, one hand turning on the radio.

She turned to see a wicker basket on the back seat, the end of a champagne bottle sticking out of it. "What in the world is that for? Isidore, I've got school work to do. I can't be away all day—"

"Can you just not make a speech for once?" he said. "How about going along with me? It isn't far."

"A picnic in October? Fine, I won't say a word. And we can go skinny dipping, too."

She sat back again, trying to look indifferent. He didn't say anything but turned on the radio. Her clip-on earring was pinching too hard so she pulled them both off and dropped them into her purse. At the start of last summer Isidore had surprised her by driving all the way to Crystal Beach. Now he was humming along to "You Send Me." Something about his calm made her more nervous. They drove up Bathurst, past St. Clair, Lawrence, Wilson, Sheppard, a long stretch of wordlessness but for the radio advertisements between the songs. The shops gave way to low apartments, and the low apartments to houses. Isidore pointed to a grassy decline and said that a new Jewish YMHA was going to be built there to serve all the families moving up from town. She put on her *isn't that interesting* face as he finally turned off Bathurst. Now they passed small brick houses with attached garages and cement porches. A couple of kids were attaching streamers to their bike handlebars and one of them stared at Miriam as they went by. Isidore halted behind a truck. Men in overalls were bringing out a sofa wrapped in plastic like a giant candy bar.

"Isidore, what exactly are we doing here?"

"You'll see." His silence was getting on her nerves. He drove another block, went left and left again. He pulled the car to the curb and turned off the engine.

"Minnie, do you know who's going to own the second half of the twentieth century?"

"I really don't know, Isidore. Walt Disney?"

"Why do you have to be so cynical?"

"You're right. I'm sorry."

"It's going to belong to Canada, that's who. Wilfrid Laurier said that and now it's true. Do you have any idea how fast the business is growing? We can hardly keep up. Three new outlets this year, and five next. Just look where things are going. Who knows where humans will be in twenty or thirty years? We could be driving in cars that float above the ground."

"I guess so. I never think about the future."

"Well, I do because I'm an optimist, Minnie. And I think that if you want something, I mean really want it, then it can come true. I read, too, you know. Speculative fiction. We're on the brink of an amazing life. People of our generation could end up living for a hundred and twenty years. And we'll still be active, we'll be playing tennis, we'll have a love life. You can't just have your head in the past, Minnie, or you'll miss everything."

"How long have you been thinking about this?"

Instead of answering, he opened the door of the car and got out. Reaching into the back, he grabbed the wicker basket. "Come on," he said and started to cross the road. She got out and followed. The houses on this end of the street were still being built. Most had their brickwork done but a couple were only wooden frames. Isidore had parked across from the one empty lot. He stepped onto it, onto the weeds and tufts of grass, went to the centre of the lot and put down the basket. He opened the flaps, took out a blanket, laid down plates and glasses. She watched him take out wrapped sandwiches that must have come from a deli, a tub of potato salad. He put the bottle between his knees and pulled the cork. He poured the foaming champagne into paper cups.

She told herself not to sound alarmed. "This is sweet, Isidore. It's also just a little crazy. I do wish you'd stop and tell me what you think you're doing."

"Sit on the blanket, Minnie. Cooperate for once in your life." She was going to object but instead kneeled down and took the offered cup. "I'm not the one who's crazy. There is going to be a swell house on this lot. A square living room with a picture window. A sunken den.

Three bedrooms. The kitchen's going to look out to the backyard over the sink. Smell the air, Minnie, it's fresh. Everything here is new and clean and modern. A school has already opened two blocks away. You know Dora and Joel Silverstein. Joel went to North Toronto. They bought the house four doors down."

"Did you buy this property, Izzy? Is that what you're telling me? Without asking me?"

"It's impossible to get a serious answer from you. It hurts, do you understand? Yes, I put a down payment on it. It's a good investment and if you don't want it I'll live here myself or I'll sell at a profit. In fact, I'm already working to get into development. I've got a large view of things, Minnie. This lot here, it's like a white sheet of paper. We can write on it whatever we want. You don't have to answer me right now, about anything. Anyway, I know you can't, or won't. So let's just drink the champagne, okay? And celebrate whatever we want. And you think about it. Think about the future, Minnie, that's all I ask. Try and imagine it for yourself and see if I'm in it."

Isidore's eyes shone. He touched his paper cup to hers and drank. She too drank, feeling the bubbles go down her throat. She choked and began to cough and then her coughs turned into crying. She didn't know why she was crying but she found that she couldn't stop and Isidore, who looked as if he had expected this exact moment, put his arm around her shoulder and let her.

§

Deborah Kersh insisted that she come with her to try out for the U.C. women's archery team.

"I've always wanted to shoot an arrow at somebody," Deborah said. They walked towards the field behind the college, where a ragged line of girls already waited. At some distance four round targets stood on easel-like stands. They were each handed a surprisingly large bow but the instructor wouldn't let them have arrows yet. She began to give them detailed instructions, most beginning with the word "Don't."

"I bet she's a lesbian," Miriam whispered.

"Well, look at those Amazonian arms."

The instructor handed an arrow to the first girl and adjusted her stance. She gave the word and the arrow flew less than halfway to the target before skidding on the grass. The next girl's shot went far to the side. Nobody hit a target. Deborah's arrow went right over them.

"I don't know my own strength," she shrugged.

"You next," said the instructor, handing Miriam an arrow. It was longer than she had expected. "No, no, if you hold it that way the fletching will rip up your fingers."

"The fletching?"

"The feathers."

She pulled back, feeling the strain in her arm. She stared at the target before her and, thinking of the catapults that lay siege to Troy in *The Iliad*, tilted upward.

Deborah leaned towards her. "Think of the backside of the professor you hate the most."

"Stand away!" barked the instructor.

She suppressed a smile and let go. The arrow whispered past her ear. It rose in a perfect arc and came down to pierce the target's outer circle.

Afterwards they went round to the lower entrance of Hart House that led to the Arbor Room. "We're waiting for our boyfriends!" Deborah announced to nobody in particular and gave Miriam a look that made her nearly burst out laughing. The room smelled of the never-empty crock of mulligatawny soup. They got porcelain cups and little clanky-metal teapots and sugar donuts and took up a corner table.

"That shot of yours was pure luck," Deborah said, taking a bite of donut.

"So you'd like to think."

"You should have seen the Amazon's face. She thought she had discovered the next Olympic champion. You were the only one she asked to come back."

"Fat chance." Miriam poured tea into her cup. "When are your parents arriving?"

"They're already here, waiting by the telephone in their motel room."

"And here you are with me? Even I'm not as awful as that."

"I know, I'm a selfish brat. It's just that when I see them my whole childhood flashes before my eyes. I could be in Sudbury again. You sure you don't want to come with me? They'd love you."

"I've really got to do some work in the library. I've done nothing for days."

Miriam looked down into her cup. She thought of telling Deborah about Isidore and the plot of land but she couldn't get herself to confess every aspect of her personal life the way other girls did. Perhaps not speaking about it made it less real. She hadn't said yes to Isidore, despite the ridiculous tears, but she hadn't said no either. Perhaps if Professor Birmingham hadn't ended her plans, but what was the use of thinking about that now? She had some unknown disease, she thought, in which her brain didn't connect to her heart, kidneys or bowel. Meanwhile Deborah, who always made a joke of her relationships, was going on about some engineering student she'd just gone on a blind date with and who spent the evening talking about cantilever bridges.

"Even I don't think I can put off the grim reapers any longer. How's my fake smile? Do I look happy and accomplished? Come on Saturday, will you, Miriam? Ta-ta, lovey."

Miriam watched her bustle between the tables and out the door. What was Saturday? She hadn't heard. She poured a little more tea and took from her purse a pocket edition of Apollinaire. The book had a silk ribbon in it and she opened to "Le pont Mirabeau."

Sous le pont Mirabeau coule la Seine
Et nos amours
Faut-il qu'il m'en souvienne
La joie venait toujours après la peine

Joy following pain — joy *needing* pain, it was such a French idea and so appealed to her. She tried to imagine herself standing on that bridge, looking down at the Seine rather than into her tepid cup of tea. In the reflection of the tea she saw the bridge, saw the buildings along the banks of the river, saw herself alone.

"Any chance you want a ticket?"

The voice made her look up. She saw a man standing by her table. "I'm sorry?"

"It's for a string quartet. My unreliable friend is a no-show so I've got an extra. But maybe you already have one."

She saw now that the room had become crowded with people. Of course, they were waiting for the concert in Hart House. Women were allowed in for that. The young man had straw hair and a long, not really handsome face, and she recognized him — or thought she recognized him — as the figure who had been asleep on the quad bench before the start of school. Of course if it was him, he wouldn't remember her, and now he was smiling in a friendly and expectant manner.

"Yes. Yes, I'd like a ticket. Thanks."

"I'm going to be nice and give it to you for free."

"But they're always free."

"Shoot, I was hoping you didn't know that."

She put away her book before taking her coat from the back of her chair. "Do you know what they're playing?"

"No idea whatsoever. But I imagine they'll start soft and get louder, and that one section will sound like a march, and another like a dirge, and another like a hymn, and then they'll swell up and end with a bang."

"I hope you're not a music major." He was trying too hard but she didn't mind. "You don't sound like you're from Toronto. Are you American?"

"I admit it. Chicago."

They went outside, where a line ran up the stone steps and through the doors. He pulled the tickets from the pocket of his long coat. "Here's yours. I don't want to force you to sit with me."

If she were Deborah, she thought, she would say something flirtatious, something like, *You don't want me to sit with you?* But she only said, "I don't mind."

"Good. You can tell me the difference between the long funny horn and the short one."

"There are no horns in a string quartet."

"See? You're helping already."

He didn't need much encouragement. The queue moved along the hall past the porter's desk to one of the long, paneled rooms. Wooden folding chairs had been set up in rows and there was a noisy clatter as people took up places. They had to settle for two near the back. The doors were closed and then opened again for the musicians to come in, a quartet of middle-aged men in black carrying their violins, viola, cello. They settled into their chairs, tuned to the first violin, there was a pause and a nod before the first stroke of a bow. She recognized Haydn, or thought she did, but didn't know the name of the piece. The only record her family had bought in the last ten years was *The King and I.* Her musical education had begun in her first year at university, when she made regular visits to the library listening booth. She regretted not having kept it up, another little failed ambition. When she looked over at the tall young man beside her, he was gazing somewhere above the musicians, not swaying exactly but moving nonetheless. Unlike her, he seemed able to stop thinking and just listen.

After Haydn came Mozart and then something she could positively identify, Dvorak's *American Quartet.* The first violin was sweetly intense and the cello beautifully echoed lower and she did lose herself, or almost, for she was conscious of doing so and of being conscious. And then it was over and they too were applauding and the crowd rose and shuffled out, the two of them seeming to accept without speaking that they were not yet parting.

On the steps outside students were lighting cigarettes. She noticed that his overcoat was missing the second button.

"I think they were very good," she said.

"Some of it reminded me of jazz, which I actually know. The way the various melodic lines played around one another. The comparison only goes so far, since jazz gives the impression of looseness and this — well, this was perfection really. Are you hungry? It's almost time for supper, I'd say. Care to get something to eat? Unless you've got something else to do."

"No, nothing," she said quickly. Her mother wanted her home, she knew, but she hadn't actually said she would make it. "It'll have to be cheap. I don't have very much money."

"Me neither. There's that little Italian place, the one with the checked table cloths."

She had expected him to offer to pay and half-flushed with embarrassment. "I know it. The one that doesn't seem to have a name. Let's go there."

They walked to Harbord Street. He asked her the usual questions: what she was studying, her family, where she lived. The restaurant was a half-basement space with small high windows that gave it a cave-like feeling. Unlit candles stood on the tables. It occurred to her that

someone she knew might be inside but there was only a
family taking up the centre table and a man eating alone
by the door, and they took a place against the back wall.
The owner greeted the tall young man by name so she
found out he was "Charlie." They ordered a carafe of house
wine and two spaghetti specials which came with a bun
and salad. The food came quickly and she watched him
eat hungrily, slurping up the long noodles. Had she even
told him her name? She took it as her turn to ask questions and he told her that he was studying architecture
but didn't like his professors, his fellow students or the
assignments. "Why does a person pick anything? When
I was a kid I liked to draw cities with a ruler and a pencil.
It was a bit of an obsession but that's my personality.
My father worked in the Chicago Savings Bank Building
and I loved when he took me to the office and I could
look out the window at the city. So here I am, in a department that's completely backwards looking. Are you going
to finish your bun? I can eat endlessly and the wind will
still blow me away. If we ask Lorenzo nicely he'll put up a
pot of espresso. Ever had one? The stuff's dynamite and
it'll keep you up half the night but I hardly sleep anyway."

His nervous energy made her uneasy. She asked
about his family and he called his parents "old Chicago
commies." All through childhood he'd been dragged to
lectures, rallies, protests. He'd lost his virginity to an older
woman at a communist picnic — "before I was ready, if

that's possible." His father had lost his bank job in '53 and now drove a cab, which he claimed to like better. "And then the whole Khrushchev thing happened, saying what a murdering bastard Stalin had been. My parents quit the party and ever since they've been like lost little lambs. It's just sad. Anyway, it was their idea I should study in Canada. I don't know if it's really much different here except for being rather dull, if you don't mind my saying so."

The espresso came, dark liquid in two tiny cups. She followed his lead in pouring in sugar and tipping it back, strong and sweet. It seemed to make her heart speed up. They counted out their money on the table and she had to cover the coffees and the tip. "*Arrivederci,* Lorenzo," he said to the owner who vaguely waved to them as he headed back into the kitchen.

It wasn't quite raining but the air was cooler and she could feel the dampness on her skin. He said that his place was on Sussex Street nearby and she claimed to need a walk and fell in step. Quickly she told him about Isidore and admitted to being "practically engaged." He listened, with an appearance of objective disinterest — perhaps she was hoping he would appear jealous. "That's the way it is these days, isn't it?" he said. "What they want for all of us. Get married, have a baby, sign the mortgage, another baby, a car, a two-week vacation and a burial plot. It's like we beat the Nazis and it gave us the right to own a washing machine. You know what I'd really like to be? A farmer.

I mean it. I don't know a goddamn thing about the land but that's what I'd like to do. In fact, you could write everything I do know on the inside of a matchbook."

"Why do you belittle yourself?" she asked. "Forgive me for saying so, but it seems disingenuous."

He laughed. "You're shrewd. I want to say it's because I'm insecure but it's more likely a feint to hide my arrogance. Well, we've reached my castle."

They stopped at a small house with a cracked window on the second floor and the skeleton of a baby carriage rusting in the small front garden. She felt a shiver of revulsion. He said, "You probably don't want to come in. But I'll ask you anyway. Although you should know that it's not as pretty inside."

"Yes, I'll come in. For a bit."

"Really?" He had a lovely smile when it was unforced. "My entrance is in the back."

They had to turn sideways to slip between houses. The back yard had been used as a dumping ground for ashes. Steps led down to a basement door. "I've forgotten my key but since the lock is broken it doesn't matter." He tapped the door open with his heel and reached in for the light pull. She followed him into the unfinished space, a few scraps of rug thrown on the cement floor. A couple of armchairs had books spilling from them. A sink was bolted to a standing pipe and a hot plate rested on a bridge table with its cord wired somewhere up above. There was a metal bedframe painted hospital green and a wardrobe with its doors covered in newspaper clippings.

"This is truly awful."

He nodded. "At least I've got a record player. But all I've got is jazz. What do you like?"

"I don't know. Dave Brubeck?"

"Sure, there's nothing wrong with him. But I don't have any so let's try something else." He leaned down and began to shift albums from one pile to the other. "Nah, nah, nah. Okay, the Gerry Mulligan Quartet. It'll suit the mood."

"What is the mood?"

"The mood I'm trying to create. Not desperate but bohemian." He put on the record and dropped the arm. A rattling drum and then a saxophone and trumpet springing over it. He stood up and walked over and kissed her on the mouth. He slipped his hand around her. She pulled away a little, but then pretended she wanted to look at him. They came together and kissed again. He moved her towards the bed. She didn't care if it felt good. She didn't care if it hurt.

"Tell me your name," he said.

§

Getting out of bed, slipping on her underpants and bra, her blouse and skirt. She didn't feel relieved or liberated or pleased with herself.

She thought that she might throw up.

He reached up from the tangle of sheets, making the bed creak. "You could stay."

"Don't be ridiculous." It was her mother's voice that had come out. She found the brush in her purse and vigorously worked at her hair without a mirror.

"My last name is Kroken," he said. "Charlie Kroken. You didn't tell me your own last name. Do you want to meet tomorrow?"

"I can't."

"Why?"

"Let me count the ways."

"It doesn't have to be a bad thing, Miriam. We can make it a good thing."

"Is that what you always do?" Why in the world did she say that? As if it were his fault, when all she wanted was for him to take her to bed. It was as if she couldn't help falling into the role expected of her. Expected by who — whom? Charlie sighed with disappointment and she wondered if that was his first disappointment in her, or if she had been less than he had hoped in bed. How could she have been anything else? He closed his eyes, putting his head down on the pillow and appearing to fall back into unconsciousness. With one heel not properly in her shoe she hobbled up from the foul basement into the trash heap of a back garden and slipped out to the street. Her skin felt sticky and vulnerable and suddenly cold. All she wanted was a bath. She was sore down there.

A Diamond cab moved along Bloor and although she had only taken one cab ride alone in her life she flagged it now. She slumped in the back, making herself small. At the corner of Eglinton she asked the driver to stop, just in case a neighbour was looking out a window. She walked past the dark houses to her own, where the porch light had been left on. She unlocked the door and slipped off her shoes to tread lightly along the hall, only to see a wan light spilling from the kitchen. The sound of a scraping chair. She had no choice but to go in.

Her mother sat at the kitchen table with a book and a glass of water and an open packet of digestives. She seemed to be staring at the sink.

"I'm sorry, Ma, I should have called."

Her mother turned and Miriam saw now that she was crying.

"Ma, what's wrong? Did something happen?"

She knelt in front of her, grasping her mother's legs.

"Oh Minnie, it's a terrible book, just terrible."

"Book? What are you reading?"

The book had been laid on the table. Miriam picked it up. On the cover was a drawing of several people standing on what looked like ice in an endlessly receding landscape.

"*On the Beach*. I've heard of it. I saw someone reading it on the bus."

"They die at the end," her mother said. "Because of a nuclear accident or war, I'm not even sure. All the characters die. Everybody on earth dies. It's so quiet, like a candle blowing out."

Miriam leaned even closer and stroked her mother's hair. She had stopped dyeing it and there were grey strands near the front. "It's just a book, Ma. It won't happen. They're making sure of that."

Her mother pushed her away.

"You smell. You smell like — never mind what. Go wash yourself."

Mortified, she walked out of the kitchen.

Let the whole world blow up right now, she thought.

§

The next week she got up early every morning and went to the library. She had lunch in the Junior Common Room, lounging with her women friends while the men as usual kept to the other side of the room. She wrote a paper on Hart Crane for modern poetry, she made a halting presentation in French on Huysmans, she attended her classes in political science and art history. What she had thought pleasingly eccentric about Professor Birmingham — his nest of a beard, his dramatic readings, the odd hum he sometimes made — she now despised. Yet she joined in a discussion on Shakespeare's late romances, vociferously disagreeing with him until his exasperation showed.

And all this time she did not see Charlie Kroken.

She came home more often. At dinner her mother gazed at her with a mixture of suspicion and concern, while her father was his usual adoring self. She made an effort to be nice to her brother as they sat in the living room watching television, getting up for the telephone ring that was Isidore's nightly call. Then she went upstairs and read in bed for a long time and turned out the light and did not see Charlie Kroken.

§

On Friday Deborah Kersh convinced her to go to a house party on Lowther Avenue. She made a batch of brownies and met Deborah at the corner of Bedford and Bloor. They weren't sure of which house it was but could hear music spilling from the open doorway as they approached. Ahead of them two men came from the other direction, carrying in a washtub of Crown & Anchors sloshing in ice water. Deborah looked good in dark slacks but Miriam still couldn't get herself to stop wearing dresses to parties. They threw off their coats and Miriam pulled the tinfoil off the brownies. She took two steps before a flurry of hands picked half of them off.

Irving and Judith and Michael surrounded them. "Lots of booze but no food so you ladies are a welcome sight," Irving said.

"My mother's a lady," Deborah said. "And you're an ass."

"These are delicious," Michael mumbled.

Little crepe paper–covered lanterns decorated the rooms. The air was dense with cigarette smoke. On the record player Lead Belly was singing "Good Night, Irene." Miriam barely knew the hosts, who had been married at city hall a week earlier. On the walls were the bride's oil paintings, which Deborah pronounced "mousey." The husband worked for an advertising agency called Locke Johnson.

"So where's your man?" Judith asked. "The hand-somely twitchy Isidore."

"He hates university parties. I don't blame him really. Last time Nathan made fun of him for never having heard of Jung. I thought Isidore was going to hit him."

"I'd like to see Nathan get hit. I'll go get us drinks; I heard there's gin in the fridge. Meanwhile, see if you can take over the record player from Norman Goetz. I want to hear the new Belafonte album."

Someone grabbed Deborah's hand and dragged her into the crowd. Miriam made her way to the back wall of the dining room, where the record player sat on a Victorian roll-top desk that had been painted blue. Norman Goetz was scrutinizing the back of a record album. He had curly hair and a beard and wore wire-frame glasses.

"Hi, Norman," she said. "I have a request."

"Nowhere on this Weavers album is the provenance of the tune given. Where's the scholarly impulse?"

"You can't just play records with banjo on them."

"Caroline Mendelsohn broke up with me. I can do what I want."

"I'm sorry to hear it. Now put on Harry Belafonte. Deborah loves that calypso beat."

"She'll have to kill me first."

"It might come to that."

"All right, I'll play one song. And then I'm putting on 'Mississippi Boweavil Blues.'"

"Very considerate of you, Norman."

When she returned there was no sign of Deborah, not even in the kitchen, so she pulled a bottle out of the washtub and used the opener tied with a string to the refrigerator door.

"The country is filled with fanatics! Do you hear me! It needs people like us, people who aren't interested in throwing grenades into the Knesset."

"I can't return to somewhere I've never been."

She went upstairs looking for a bathroom, having to work her way around people sitting on the steps. But when she tried the bathroom door it was locked. Giggling came from inside. So she came down again and found her jacket and went outside.

Walking away, she could feel herself breathe again. Dry leaves trembled overhead. On a front porch on Huron

Street two old men in sweaters were playing chess by the light of a kerosene lamp. She pretended not to know where she was going, a necessary game even if she wasn't fooling herself in the slightest. What a surprise to have reached Sussex.

There were no lights on in the main part of the house and she wondered if anyone lived in it. Slipping between the houses to the back it became almost pitch-black. She reached the ashy yard and quickly knocked on the door.

"Charlie?"

She pushed the door open and waved her hand above her head until she touched the light pull. The bulb cast a wan light over the row of shirts hanging from an overhead pipe and the broken-down armchairs. She called again even though she could feel he wasn't there. The sink was full; why weren't men brought up to look after themselves? She couldn't stop herself from washing up, stacking the plates and cups and cutlery on a crate. She tossed empty cans into the garbage bin and picked up stray clothes. The hanging shirts were dry and since there was no iron she folded and placed them in the wardrobe.

Closing the wardrobe door, she saw the newspaper clippings tacked onto it. There were grainy photographs of young Negroes grouped around a sofa or standing with schoolbooks in their hands. *A Test for Nine Arkansas Kids. National Guard Fails to Maintain Order. Eisenhower Sends in 101st Airborne Division.* Of course she knew who they were, those high school kids in Little Rock, Arkansas, the first Negroes allowed to go to the white school. Even the Toronto papers were full of the story. She looked more closely at the photographs, counting six girls and three boys. One of the boys was tall and almost handsome but for too-big ears. One of the girls was really striking. She couldn't help appraising their dresses — were they home-made? Crouching lower, she examined a photograph of one Negro girl in sunglasses with books under her arm while a mob of white people screamed at her. There was one particular white girl, just behind, screaming murder as if she might do something violent. But the Negro girl looked brave and dignified.

Of course it was an awful situation, surely any decent person would think so. Still, she wondered why Charlie had cut the articles out and used the wardrobe as a bulletin board. It wasn't as if his people were involved. And he was from Chicago, not Arkansas.

"Come home, Charlie," she whispered. Suddenly she felt so tired, like Goldilocks in the bears' house. She went to his unmade bed, straightened it, and lay down on her back with her hands clasped and closed her eyes. She couldn't even pretend to know what she was doing.

§

She was awakened by his lips touching hers. She wrapped her arms around his neck and drew him down to the bed.

"What time is it?"

"Late. How long have you been here?"

"Years."

"Well, thank you."

"For what?"

"For sleeping in my bed."

She wanted to say, *Please fuck me,* but couldn't get the words out. She didn't have to as he began to unbutton her dress. From his jacket pocket he took out a box and held it up to her. *Champ Prophylactics,* with a picture of a baseball player. She felt as touched as if he had brought her roses. They took their time and it didn't hurt so much and then it felt all right and then if not good almost good and he pressed his hands into the bed beside her and arched his long back, looking as if he was having a religious experience. Then he slumped and laughed gently and kissed her all over and she was sorry he was done.

To herself she said, this has to, has to, has to be the last time.

And out loud, "I was looking at those newspaper clippings on the door."

"Ah. The door of shame."

He began to tell her about other incidents — a Negro woman who tried to enter the University of Alabama, a high school in Tennessee. Little Rock was just the most prominent and dramatic, he said, the one that the press had decided to write about. Growing up, his parents had always talked to him about civil rights and inequality; they were central to the Communist critique of American society. That's what had made the most impression on him, rather than all that praise of the Soviet system. Last year he and some Jewish friends had formed a civil rights group to go down to Montgomery, Alabama, during the bus boycott, although they hadn't really done much but hand out sandwiches. And now there were these incredible kids who just wanted to go to the best high school in their city. And here he was stuck in Canada, just as his mother and father had wanted, far from where he might do something. He spoke the names of the kids aloud as if he knew them personally. Gloria Ray, Ernest, Thelma, Minnijean, Melba, Carlotta, Jefferson, Terrence, Elizabeth.

As he spoke he seemed to go somewhere else, to be far away from her. But then he reached under the sheet and took her hand.

§

Anyone who has a secret, she thought, lives in two worlds. And the world that is new (for the secret world is always new) has a depth and a glow and trembling life that the regular, everyday world can never match.

She skipped a day of classes to stay with him in the bed of his ruined palace.

She went home and talked to her parents just as she always did, and looked with genuine interest at Brian's scrapbook, and waited for Isidore to pick her up, and said she wasn't feeling well and could he take her home early.

And she went again. And felt for the first time something more powerful than anything she had ever imagined. It wasn't worship of him, peculiar and imperfect man that he was. She knew it was about her. And it was not without pain. It was a delicious cut that she caressed over and over so that it wouldn't heal.

§

Along Eglinton Avenue: the Honey Dew Restaurant, the Skirt 'n Sweater Shop, Kalifer Furs. It had been as comfortable and safe as a village, and when she was a child walking with her parents, people they knew had always stopped to say how big she was getting, or how pretty, or what a nice dress she had on. And then it was the first place she was allowed to go on her own, fourteen years old with Faiga Lasky giggling at her side, going for ice cream or a matinee at the movie house.

And now she walked with her father, who had woken her up at noon on Sunday, knocking loudly on her door and saying that it was a crime to sleep in so late. So she had dragged herself out of bed and doused her face in cold water, and put on makeup. Her father had been waiting downstairs in his suit and tie and hat, his overcoat on his arm. And now, just as if she were a little girl again, people nodded or stopped to say hello and ask what she was doing and how was her mother. They even ran into Mrs. Lasky. "Did you know that Faiga is coming home for Yom Kippur? She's bringing the baby, of course. I was speaking to her on the phone last night and she told me to make sure that Minnie knew. She expects a visit as soon as she arrives."

"Consider the message delivered," her father said. "We'll drop by sometime, too. Of course we want to see the baby."

Her father touched his hat and they walked on. "You didn't look so enthusiastic about seeing Faiga." He sniffed the air. "I think maybe winter is coming early."

"You're a chiropodist *and* a weatherman."

"I see you don't want to answer."

"No, I really do want to see Faiga. It's just that we're not kids anymore. We don't really have anything in common."

"I don't know what's not to have in common. You can make new friends, Minnie, but there's nothing like old friends. They know you the way nobody else does. Look at me and Fred Shepsy."

"You never see Fred Shepsy."

"That isn't the point. You want a cup of tea? I could use one."

They were standing outside the Noshery. It was always crowded on Sunday and there were several families waiting for tables, but the elderly waitress took them to a small table by the kitchen doors.

"This is all you have?" her father asked.

"You see anything else? I can put you back in line, it's no skin off my nose."

"At least we'll get a breeze from that door opening every two minutes. Two orders of tea and two pieces of poppyseed cake."

"I'm really not hungry," Miriam said.

"You don't need to be hungry to eat something sweet. You're small to begin with and I think you've lost weight. Actually, it's your mother who noticed. Look at me, for years I wore the same size as when I was a young man. And now practically every year your mother needs to let out my trousers. And already you're back?" he said as the waitress put down their order. "The tea bag isn't even in the pot. Would you serve the queen this way?"

"She hasn't come in yet."

The waitress left. "This is no longer a British country," her father said. She waited for the tea to steep, moving the piece of cake with her fork. She found it hard to look at her father and wished that she hadn't agreed to come. Every few months he liked to have a talk with her in order to know what was really going on, as he put it, and she could feel him on the verge of asking now. She poured her tea and took a sip.

"So tell me," he said, "how are the studies?"

"They're okay."

"Just okay? I know how important they are to you."

"They're fine."

"I admire how you go into things. The seriousness of it. Studying literature, it isn't something I took much notice of. I wanted a good profession, something to be respected for. I didn't want to work myself into the grave like my father with nothing to show for it. He helped to pay for my schooling in Baltimore and before I graduated he was dead. But I found a calling. I help people who are suffering and I make a decent living for my family. But you have a different sort of mind. Deeper."

"I don't know about that."

"I do. It's not as if I thought you enjoyed working in the office this summer."

"It wasn't so bad."

"You hated it. But that's fine, I want you to find what you're suited for."

"Can we talk about something else?"

She put out her hand to cover his. He looked up at her. "Of course, sweetheart. It's just nice to sit with you."

"Don't you have to pick Brian up from Hebrew school?"

"The Gorshans are going to bring him home. We alternate now, it's easier. And your mother is hoping that Brian and the Gorshan boy will become friends." He sighed and put a square of cake into his mouth. "Anyway, it hasn't happened yet."

"How about we talk about you?" Miriam said. "I thought you and Mom were finally going to go on a holiday."

"Maybe we discussed it. Or maybe your mother did and I listened."

"Why don't you go to Miami Beach over Christmas?"

"Or maybe the moon."

"I know you can afford it. And Mom would love to go. I hear those beach hotels are spectacular. You can lie in the sun, eat in the restaurant. Actually relax for a change. Just the two of you without responsibilities."

"It's true your mother deserves it. And I would like to see the ocean. But the question is Brian. If we take him, we'll spend the whole holiday doing what he wants. But I don't see how we can leave him. If he had friends to stay with, that would be different. Or if he would make friends in the hotel."

He picked up his tea cup, careful not to look at her. Of course it was Miriam herself he was thinking of, Miriam the only one who could take care of Brian. A month ago, two weeks even, she might have felt generous enough to say yes, even if she would have regretted it later. But now her breath came rapidly and she felt trapped in this chair, across from her father, in this restaurant —

"It doesn't matter," her father said quickly. "Eat your cake, sweetheart. Listen, we're thinking of going to the early show tonight. Brian wants to see *Old Yeller.* Maybe you'll come."

If it was the early show, she could still go out afterwards. "Sure," she said. "That would be nice."

§

He had long, narrow feet and his little toes were like commas.

A discoloured crescent on his thigh remembered a tent pole falling at a socialist youth camp in the Adirondacks.

His spare chest hair was reddish blonde.

His knees were sensitive.

A bit of green sometimes caught in the gap between his lower front teeth.

After handball games with another architecture student he never dried himself properly, so that his shirt clung damply.

He was either content to remain silent or wouldn't shut up. He tore paper napkins in his hands without realizing it. He sometimes gently mocked her for having bourgeois assumptions. When he became excited or nervous his childhood stutter returned.

It was possible, he said once, that he cared more about jazz than social justice. On the street he found a five-dollar bill and immediately used it to buy a Charlie Parker album.

He was attracted to Buddhism but thought he was too attached to the self and the world.

Knowing him became her subject matter. She had trouble focusing on her course work, which seemed now irrelevant. Charlie, though, appeared to do no work at all. A half-built model of a Frank Lloyd Wright–style house was overdue yet sat untouched on the basement floor. One afternoon she came by to pick up her scarf, only to find him lying on the bed with his hands behind his head. He jumped up and started going on about how Eisenhower might pull the soldiers out of Little Rock, leaving Arkansas' dubious National Guard to protect the nine teenagers. How were those kids going to get into school? Who was going to stop the white kids from spitting on them, or kicking them, or cracking their skulls?

"Yes, that is terrible," she said. "But aren't you supposed to be writing an exam at this moment?"

"Who's going to care if not us? I mean, haven't you been called a dirty Jew? Gone to a restaurant where suddenly there were no empty tables? We all know which clubs we can't join, which colleges have a quota, which firms won't hire us. Or maybe it hasn't affected you. Naturally a girl who's been spoiled and protected her whole life —"

She, who never resorted to tears, began to cry. Immediately he came over and put his arms around her.

"Of course I know it," she said. "Sometimes it's worse, the things men think they can say to me."

"I'm sorry, I got carried away. I can be so self-righteous sometimes. Forgive me."

She began to unbutton his shirt.

§

She spent a whole Saturday with Charlie and then went home to put on a new dress and waited for Isidore to pick her up.

Brian had his box of toy soldiers out and because they couldn't stand up on carpeting, he had laid out four record albums in a square for his battlefield.

She knew that she had to tell Isidore that she wasn't going to marry him. She tried to imagine telling him tonight.

Car headlights lit up the front curtains. She stepped over the record albums, knocking over several soldiers and setting Brian off. She thought he was too old to have tantrums and that they were another sign something was wrong with him. Quickly she helped to set the soldiers upright again and then called out to her parents. She heard her mother come walking towards the stairs and hurried out the front door so as not to see her.

The car windows were partly open and music spilled out. In the back seat she could see Isidore's best friend, Stanley, with his new girlfriend. Isidore leaned over to throw open the door for her.

"Can't you just let me tell our story without being interrupted?" Stanley was saying. "You can listen, too, Minnie. So I took my dad's car down to the CNE. You know how hard it is to park — people let you use their front lawns for a small ransom. So I thought I was smart because I squeezed just off the road between two cars. But when I came back some jackass had poured a chocolate malt over the hood. I knew my father would have a conniption fit so I drove over to Farb's. You know, the car wash at King and Beverly."

"King and John," said Isidore, keeping his eyes on the road.

"Fine. So I leave the car for a wash and wax and saunter across the road to kill time. And I see an office with a sign. Wait, you tell me, big shot, since you think you know this town so well."

Isidore didn't hesitate. "Authors and Cox, sellers of artificial limbs and trusses."

"You're like an *idiot savant*. Anyway, I'm about to keep walking when I look past the display of wooden legs in the window and see this beautiful girl sitting at a desk."

"That would be me," said Lauren, the new girlfriend.

"That's right, babe. I go in through the door, looking around like I'm really interested in the inventory, and find myself up at the desk just as the beautiful girl is hanging up the phone. And I say to her — honey, tell them what I said to you."

"Oh, please."

"I said, 'Hey, baby, I'd really go out on a limb for you, real *or* artificial.' Didn't I, babe?"

"You and the twelve other guys who came in before. But for some reason I laughed when you said it. I think it was the way you batted your eyelashes. Boy do I regret it. You know the kind of regret I'm talking about, Minnie. By the way, we haven't met."

"A pleasure," Miriam said. "Where exactly are we going?"

"Mutual Street," Isidore answered, turning smoothly down Yonge.

"Really? We haven't done that in ages."

Miriam looked out at the dark shops and occasional squat apartment building. Lauren and Stanley kept talking; they were good at filling the space left by her and Isidore. The car slid down Yonge, past Bloor Street and the mean taverns, past Eaton's and Simpson's. They turned onto Mutual Street and parked the car in the lot across from the arena that looked like a brick factory. The men paid for them at the window and they joined the line for the roller skate rentals. Inside, the benches were lined with people putting on skates. She pulled on hers and tied the long laces and then the four of them stood against the boards watching the skaters going round the oval track to Bill Haley and His Comets playing from the tinny speakers.

"Shall we?" asked Stanley, putting out his arm. He and Lauren stepped onto the cement floor. Stanley's feet immediately went out from under him and he pulled her down with him. They got up, half-laughing and half-arguing and slowly set off.

"That could be us," Isidore said.

"Looking like clowns, you mean?"

"Having a good time. Sounding like an actual couple."

She felt herself grow tense. But she took his arm and looked up into his face and gave a slight smile, knowing she looked pretty that way. "Come, Isidore. Skate with me."

They joined the flow of bodies and she felt her skirt flutter against her legs. Suddenly she wanted to go faster. Isidore neatly matched her stride. She started to breathe harder; it felt good. Perhaps, she thought, life only gave the appearance of forward movement, when in reality it was merely a sequence of still images. And these moments, each separate, they didn't add up, didn't have a causal relationship and therefore consequence, and she could take this moment on its own, for what it was and no more, pushing off with her right leg, and now her left. They went around twice this way and then slowed and Isidore put his hands on her waist and she gasped as he lifted her into the air.

§

Brian was screaming in his room. From the living room they could hear him stamping his feet and throwing things.

"He better not break that new globe," her father said.

He was being punished for cutting pictures out of *Time,* which had arrived in the mail that day. He had used scissors to snip out three colour photographs of an Atlas rocket being launched. When it had gone off course, the air force had blown it up in the air — that was the photograph Brian had liked best. In disgust, her father had left the magazine on the coffee table and she had picked it up. The cover story, "Paratroopers in Little Rock," described President Eisenhower's difficult decision and gave a profile of the governor of Arkansas, whom the reporter clearly considered a demagogue and opportunist. There was a description of the soldiers escorting the nine teenagers into the high school along with photographs of people pushing at the barriers set up. Did they have any idea how ugly they looked? The Negro teenagers looked so calm and studious in comparison.

"He's going to make himself sick," said her mother. She walked to the stairs with the slowness of one condemned to being the parent of a child impossible to save.

Miriam said, "I'm going out."

"With Isidore?"

"With school friends. We're going to study together."

"Next week is Yom Kippur," her father said, undoing his tie.

"I know."

"We're going to schul."

"I said I know, didn't I?"

It was cold out. She wore a tan beret, which didn't do much to keep her warm. On the bus she rehearsed what she would say about the article in *Time*, how Governor Faubus was talking about abolishing the public school system as a way around the law and how meanwhile some white kids in the cafeteria had asked one of the Negro boys to sit with them. At last she was walking quickly on Sussex to the decrepit house that had become her favourite place in the world.

Charlie himself was sidling between the two houses.

"Aren't we going in? I'm chilled." And into his ear, "I want to go to bed."

He kissed her but said, "I have to get out of there. I feel like a caged animal. I need to get out of my head, too. Do you mind going out?"

"No," she lied but then just as quickly it was the truth. They had been out in public so rarely. Usually she worried about running into someone she knew, but right now she couldn't have cared less. They walked to College Street where Charlie hailed a cab, which took them almost the same route as Isidore had driven her two nights ago, down Yonge Street. But instead of turning they went a little farther, until he told the driver to pull up.

Getting out, she saw the illuminated sign of the Colonial Tavern. It looked as if it had been squashed between to old bank buildings. "I miss Chicago," Charlie said, coming up beside her. "It's the next best thing, I guess." She followed him inside, into the dark and with jazz music spilling towards them, and while her eyes were still adjusting he paid the cover charge and reached for her hand. The long room was about half-full. He led her to a table not far from the front and the waiter came and took their order for two beers. Charlie turned his chair and already he was smiling, his shoulders moving to the rhythm. She looked to the stage and saw five Negro musicians. They wore pinstripe suits with white shirts and black ties and they swayed as they played. They had chairs but the two horn players, the trumpet and trombone, along with the clarinet player, were standing up, with the double bass player and drummer behind them. Of course she'd seen jazz before, but they were always big bands playing dance music and the musicians had all been white.

She leaned towards him. "Do you know the song?"

"Uh-huh. 'Savoy Blues.' It's a Louis Armstrong tune. The drummer's especially good, don't you think?"

The drummer? She hadn't taken much notice. When the song ended the applause was loud and the musicians grinned as if they themselves were having the best time in the world. She began to say, "I was reading *Time*" when they started playing again. She recognized the tune as "I Love Paris" but as an instrumental. The beat was so infectious she expected couples to get up and dance but nobody did.

They played three more songs to the end of the set. Then Charlie got up and walked to the stage and shook hands with each of the musicians in turn. The trumpet player, a lean young man with his hair cut close to his scalp, knelt down and put his hand on Charlie's shoulder for a moment as he smiled brilliantly. Charlie looked excited but also at ease in a way she could never be.

He returned to the table and dropped into his chair. "Man, I needed that. But we can go now if you want."

She put her hand on his arm. "No," she said. "Let's stay."

§

Her family attended Goel Tzedec on University Avenue, a Moorish-style building with twin domes and a mosaic over the three broad doors. Andrei Unterman came with them but then kept his distance, finding a seat near the back. Her father preferred to sit up close while she and her mother went up to the women's balcony. Brian went with his father until he got bored and came upstairs, whining until their mother agreed to take him home.

Miriam remained in the semi-dark, surrounded by women who whispered to one another more than they followed the service below. By midday the fasting was already making her feel a little light-headed. She half-dozed for a while, opening her eyes with a jerk and turning to see Faiga Lasky come in. Mrs. Lasky was behind her holding the baby. They didn't see her and took seats on the other side of the balcony. Miriam kept her head turned to the side. For years and years she and Faiga had told each other everything. They had argued, had refused to speak to one another for days, had dramatically made up again. As teenagers they had gone to the park in the evenings to swing back and forth and talk about boys and marriage but also about glamorous jobs in fashion or magazines. And now Faiga lived in Winnipeg and had her own house and maybe she was as happy as they had expected to be.

She managed to slip out the opposite door and down to the lobby where people milled about. Andrei was standing on the steps outside, watching the traffic go by. She knew that the holidays were hard and she stayed behind him until he turned around. For a moment he seemed to look right through her.

Her father came down and they all went home together. Andrei had stashed a bunch of carnations in the cloakroom for her mother and he carried them in one hand. As soon as they arrived, her mother began bringing dishes out to the table. When they sat down she felt weak with hunger. As always they started with soup, which her mother believed easiest on an empty stomach.

Afterwards, she insisted that her mother sit in the living room while she cleaned up. Andrei joined her in the kitchen where they stacked dishes in the washer and scrubbed pans.

"Miriam," Andrei said. He was standing beside her at the sink. "I feel obliged to mention that I saw you the other day."

"Mmm." She dried another pan.

"That is, I saw you with a man. Coming out of a restaurant. And you stopped and were intimate. I mean you kissed."

She felt her cheeks flush. "That's nothing. You misunderstand. He's just someone at school."

"You're are a grown woman, Miriam. But I felt if I didn't say anything I'd be deceiving you. Also I want you to know that I am your friend. If you ever need me."

"Why would I possibly need you?" She turned and smiled and handed him a pot. "And really, Andrei, I've been meaning to tell you, carnations are the ugliest flowers in the world."

He began drying the pot. "Thank you for telling me. I won't buy them again."

§

She picked up her coat from the rack in the vestibule. "Good," said her mother. "Now you can go see Faiga."

"I'm meeting friends."

Actually, she was on her way to the house on Sussex.

Her mother said, "Faiga is leaving tomorrow. Her mother called me this afternoon to ask why you haven't been over. She says Faiga is so hurt that it's all she's talking about. Your best friend! I don't know what's come over you but you're going over right now and that's all there is to it."

"We were friends as kids," Miriam said. "We don't play house anymore."

"She asked you to be the maid of honour at her wedding."

And so she sighed audibly and put on her coat and went out the door. For a moment she considered walking down the sidewalk and not stopping. She had become so good at dissembling; she did it with her parents every day. But her mother would no doubt hear about it and besides, it really did seem too mean. She stepped over the little decorative fence that separated the lawns and went up the steps of the porch to knock on the door.

Through the octagonal window she saw Faiga appear in the hallway, the baby in her arms, and when she saw Miriam through the glass she started. But she was smiling when the door opened even as she put her finger to her lips.

"He just went to sleep," she whispered. Miriam followed Faiga in and watched as she put the infant into the crib in the living room. Faiga took Miriam's hand and led her to the kitchen table.

"Oh Min, it's so good to see you. I really thought you were avoiding me. I guess I still do. I'm not interesting enough for you anymore."

"No, no," Miriam said, painfully aware that she had often thought that very thing. "It's just a bad time right now. I'm swamped with tests and essay deadlines. But I wouldn't have let you go without seeing you."

"You look so great, Minnie. So slim. And there's just something about you. Look at me! I still haven't lost all the weight. I never have time to get my hair styled."

"You're glowing, Faiga. And the baby's beautiful."

"Already that kid has personality. I love him so much it hurts. But it's hard, too. He wants, wants, all the time. I'm so glad the doctor convinced me to switch to a bottle because he was sucking the life out of me. I know he's going to be a handful when he gets older. But still, he's so wonderful, I don't have the words for it. I wanted you to see him. I need you to know that everything we used to talk about has come true."

"You sit, I'll make us tea," Miriam said, standing up. She filled the kettle at the sink. "How is Winnipeg? It just seems so far away."

"You promised me you'd visit, remember? All right, even I wouldn't ask you to come in the winter. It's like the North Pole. But the summer is really nice — once the mosquitoes are gone. We have such terrific neighbours — right next door is a mom with two kids, Jewish. Her name is Toby and she reminds me of you, I think that's why I became friends with her so fast. She's funny and she reads a lot. She belongs to the Book-of-the-Month Club. There are parties, too, only now we hardly ever go because my mother-in-law doesn't like to babysit if you can believe it. Len is really working hard but it's a great time to be in his business, people want security for their families. Oh, look who doesn't want to miss the fun."

The baby had started to make noises some time ago, a distressing sound to Miriam, but Faiga had ignored it until now. The noises turned to crying and Faiga got up and scooped him from the crib. Did it mean something, that she could never remember the child's name? And was there something wrong with her if she didn't want a baby?

But perhaps she did want a baby.

And she thought: it'll be too late to see Charlie.

Faiga put a bottle up to warm. "Now tell me what's going on with you, Min. Do you still like college so much? What happens after you finish? Will you get a job? I know from your mom that Isidore is still in the picture. I can't believe he hasn't popped the question yet."

It was the moment she had dreaded. She could tell her old friend what was really happening to her, could take the risk and hope that Faiga, who had always been so understanding, would not judge her, at least not too harshly. Their friendship might end but it might be renewed or even strengthened. She would have someone to talk to, to help her make sense of what she was doing. But even as she considered all this she knew that she wouldn't share Charlie with Faiga.

"Really," she said, "there's almost nothing to tell."

Faiga's expectant look changed. Her smile vanished and her jaw clenched as she looked away. But then she got up for the bottle and, smiling at the baby, said, "Who's my handsome boy?"

§

Brian refused to come out of his room. He had been so excited by the launch of *Sputnik 2* with Laika inside, pasting all the newspaper articles he could find into his scrapbook. But there were no photographs of the dog's triumphant return, no ticker-tape parade, because Laika hadn't come back. The Soviet scientists said that she had been euthanized before the oxygen ran out, but some American scientists asserted that she had died horribly from the excessive heat.

"Enough is enough," said Miriam's father. They were sitting at the table, the dishes growing cold. Miriam could see the worry behind her father's façade of anger; still he got up, strode up the stairs and banged on Brian's door with the flat of his hand. Her mother sat at the table as if made of stone.

"In this house we have dinner together, do you understand? Going to space is a waste of money. Besides, there are millions of dogs. Why is there even a lock on this door? Come out of there."

But Brian wouldn't and, after changing to pleas and bribes, her father returned to the table.

"I have an idea," Miriam said.

"I don't think he will listen to you." Her mother could hardly get the words out.

"You don't think I know that? I'm going to phone Andrei."

"We can't call Andrei every time Brian has a tantrum," her father said.

"Well, we can call him now."

She went into the kitchen to use the telephone. Among the list of numbers taped to the side of the cupboard was the one for Andrei's boarding house. She dialed and when his miserable landlady picked up, she asked to speak to Mr. Unterman. There was a huff of annoyance and then a long wait before he came on.

"Can you come for dinner? We need help with Brian."

"Of course. Believe me, I'm glad for the dinner."

"Take a cab. My father will pay the driver."

She took the money from her father and came out to the curb when the cab pulled up. "What's wrong?" he asked, getting out.

"Brian has locked himself in his room. He's upset about a dead dog."

"A dead dog? Oh, of course."

"Maybe you can talk to him."

"Certainly I'll try."

They went into the house and she took his coat. Her father stood up but found nothing to say.

"If you'll excuse me," Andrei said, nodding as he headed for the stairs.

"Two more minutes and we eat," her father said.

They waited ten minutes, twenty. A half hour went by before they heard Brian's door open. The sound of footsteps overhead and then on the stairs. Andrei and Brian came in, the young man's hand on the boy's shoulder. Miriam and her mother brought out the dishes.

"Laika was a brave dog," Andrei said. He looked pointedly at Mr. Moscowitz.

"Yes," her father said. "He was very brave."

Miriam passed around a platter. For the second day in a row she would not be able to see Charlie. She would go tomorrow afternoon, when neither of them had classes. She looked at her brother, who was bringing a trembling fork to his mouth. She wondered if the memory of this dog was going to somehow mark him for life.

§

In the Junior Common Room she was eating a bran muffin and idly reading the names of past student presidents painted in gold letters on the wainscoting. At the other end was a stone fireplace and the grouping of sofas where the men habitually gathered. She walked over to where

Nathan, Michael, Irving and someone she didn't know were drinking coffee.

"Have you ever read the names on the walls?"

"Whatever for?" asked Nathan.

"Do you know there's never been a woman president?"

"Of the United States? I would hope not," said Michael.

"It really isn't funny."

"It's a little funny," Irving said. "Since we're on the subject, you know where the best-looking women are?"

"Nursing," said the one she didn't know. "I always go to their dances. They're completely wild. It's the blood and guts they have to see."

"You really are idiots."

"Come on, Miriam, we're just joking around."

She walked out the room, down the hall and into the cold afternoon. She didn't button her coat or take the scarf from her bag. She had thought of them as all in this together — the common pursuit, Leavis had called it. And had she ever really been taken seriously? Quickly she walked along Hoskin Avenue, past the old houses and university buildings, and turned up Huron. Charlie would just be getting back from his own class, if he went in the first place. It felt as if she would lose her mind if she didn't see him.

She got to the house and slipped between the walls and pushed open the door.

Even in the dark it felt different. She reached up for the light pull, couldn't find it for a moment, and a panicky feeling rose in her. Her fingers touched the cord and she turned it on.

His things were gone. No clothes on the pipes or the floor, the books gone, too. Also the toothbrush and razor that had lain on the edge of the sink. There were a few empty boxes, a pile of newspapers, a milk crate of empty bottles. The newspaper clippings remained on the wardrobe.

She called out, "Charlie," but in a soft voice, to fill the emptiness. Then she moved somehow to the bed and saw a torn sheet of lined paper on the pillow. *Miriam. Can't be here anymore while others struggle. xox*. She sat on the edge and began to cry. The crying grew violent, sobs jaggedly rising as if to pull out her insides. And what was she crying for? Was she crying for him, for herself? She didn't know but she couldn't stop.

But finally she did stop. She felt wrung out, the way one did after being sick to one's stomach. She washed her face in the sink and fixed her hair and lipstick. She walked out of the basement and got to Bathurst Street as the streetcar's metal wheels were grinding to a stop. She looked out the window as she had so many times, got off as she had so many times, walked to her house and took her key from the bag and let herself in.

Her mother's shoes were in the vestibule and her coat on the hanger but she wasn't in the kitchen and when Miriam crept upstairs her parents' bedroom door was shut. Her mother must have been having one of her migraines and was lying with the curtain closed and a compress over her eyes. Miriam slipped into her own room and pulled an overnight case from the closet. It was round and covered in blue vinyl and she had loved it when her father bought it for her years before, although now it struck her as ridiculous. She lay it on the bed and put in a few underthings, a sweater, shoes, a fabric toiletries kit. In her drawer was an envelope of bills and she put them in her purse. She grabbed the first book that came to hand, the small hardcover volume of *The Ambassadors* that she still hadn't read, and fit it into her purse.

She went downstairs. On the kitchen counter was a coffee can where her mother kept money for small expenses and she emptied it into her purse. She wrote a note on the shopping pad.

Don't worry, I'll let you know where I am.

She left the house.

§

There were four identical gleaming buses parked in the bays along Edward Street. She pulled open the glass door and entered the station, where men sat on wooden benches with their hats pulled down, leather sample cases by their feet. A couple of sailors in uniform stood by their duffel bags, smoking. A woman with two children clinging to her skirt was rifling through her bag.

Miriam got in line, her overnight case beside her. The man in front was perusing the racing sheet. A person would move to one of the two tellers and the line would shuffle forward. She got to the head of the line, hoping she would get the man on the left rather than the right. She got the right.

"Destination?"

"Little Rock, Arkansas."

She thought he might give her a look but his eyes stayed down as he pulled a schedule from the pile. "Gray Coach will take you to Detroit. Then you'll need to buy a ticket on the Greyhound line. Looks to me like you'll go through St. Louis and maybe Memphis but they'll be able to advise you better. The bus to Detroit leaves in twenty minutes. Bay number four."

"Yes, that's fine."

"Four dollars and fifteen cents."

He reached up to pull a ticket and slid it towards her. She put the ticket into her purse and then went to the cigarette stand and bought a package of waffle creams. She sat on a bench.

A man sat on the bench next to her. "That's some weather," he said.

She looked through the windows; it got dark so early this time of year. Rain began to streak the windows.

The man moved towards her. "I was wondering if you'd like to have a drink. Or we could go for dinner, even. I'm staying just over at the Royal York."

She got up and began to walk away before she remembered her overnight case so she had to go back for it. At the bay the bus was already parked, but the door was closed and the driver in his uniform was drinking coffee from a paper cup. She joined the line and took the book from her purse and opened it and made herself read.

A hydraulic whoosh made her start. The line moved forward, she stepped up into the bus, the driver punched her ticket. She went to the back and stood on her toes to push her case overhead before sliding into the window seat. The driver started the engine and they sat idling another few minutes before pulling out of the bay.

She tore open the package and began to eat a waffle cream as the bus rolled along the lakeshore. They passed factories and silos and picked up speed and the rain came down harder, obscuring the view. She ate three more waffle creams and then two more and then she finished the package and felt sick. But the bus rolled on, the enormous wipers moving slowly back and forth over the wide windshield.

"Port Credit," the driver announced and they pulled into the small station. She got out to wait her turn in the bathroom and promptly threw up into the toilet. She washed her face and got back onto the bus.

The rain was slanting down against the other side of the bus. Through her window she could sometimes glimpse a house or a few acres of farm against a line of trees. Her stomach felt a little more settled and she began to read again. When next she looked up they were passing a heap of rusting cars and a gas station and some kind of factory. The driver stopped in Oakville and then Burlington where she got out and bought a Coca-Cola. They pulled back onto the highway and the rain was steady and quiet so she could see only the passing headlights and the blur of a lit window in the distance. Other passengers began to fall asleep, their heads lolling.

She asked herself whether Charlie would be glad to see her or whether he would stare with annoyance or, worse, without recognition. She imagined him sitting among a group of handsome and well-dressed Negroes, engaged in an intense but civil argument about tactics. He would ask what she was doing there and she'd have to have an answer. And they would nod in approval or laugh in derision.

The bus stopped again, a good thing because the Coke had made her desperate to pee. The washroom was disgusting but she held herself above the seat.

The bus turned northwest, away from the lake and towards Brantford and Woodstock and London and Chatham. She read her book and grew drowsy and leaned the side of her face against the chilly window.

When she jolted awake and looked outside, the rain had stopped. They were on a suspension bridge which meant that the lights ahead of them were Detroit.

The bus passed some men standing around a metal trash can with flames rising from it, then a parked van with other men tossing newspaper bundles to the ground.

She heard music spilling from an open door.

The bus pulled around the Greyhound terminal, a corner building with windows that wrapped around the side and a store called Cunningham's on the ground floor. They came to a stop and the driver called out, "Deetroit," and the passengers roused themselves. Nobody offered to help get her case down so she had to stand on the edge of the seat to reach high enough.

In the terminal an old Negro man in overalls was using a wide broom to sweep sawdust along the floor. She went to the ticket counter. A man in a green visor was sorting tickets. "Little Rock, Arkansas, please."

"You sure, Miss? A lot of trouble there just now."

"Yes, I'm sure."

"Suit yourself. I can give you a ticket for Louisville, with a change at Dayton. Then it's Nashville and a straight ride to Memphis. From there it's another hundred and fifty miles or so to Little Rock. Take you a couple of days once you get started. The bus to Dayton leaves in the morning. Ten a.m."

"There's nothing tonight?"

"I would have told you if there was. You won't have any trouble getting on, that's not a busy route. You can buy your ticket when you come back."

"All right, thank you."

Miriam picked up her case and walked across the floor. She went out the glass door and she stood on a street called Washington Boulevard as a stream of cars went by. Not far ahead she could see brick buildings that looked like hotels and she began walking in that direction.

She kept her case close and it bumped against her leg. The buildings faced a dark circle that must have been grass and they were hotels but as she got closer she knew they would be too expensive given how much money she carried. And so she turned in the other direction and kept her eyes straight because she didn't want to know if any of the people she passed were looking at her.

She stopped in front of the Hotel Ross. It was six storeys of dull brick, with three steps leading up to a single door. Through the glass she could see the small lobby with two armchairs and a young man behind the counter reading a book. She opened the door and went in, hearing a radio turned low. A contestant made an answer and there was a burst of laughter. As she came forward the young man put down his paperback, called *Violent Saturday*, and looked up.

"Do you have a room available?"

"We've got a women-only floor. There's a corner room with a sink. The bathroom is down the hall. It's five dollars a night, payment in advance."

"Yes, I'll take it." She opened her purse.

"We don't have an elevator."

He handed her the oversized key and pointed to the stairs. She went up three floors and then along a hall lit in a series of overlapping circles by the yellow wall lamps. She opened the door to a square room with two windows, neither of which had a view. She went down the hall to the toilet and came back to the room where she brushed her teeth and washed her face. There was a small square of towel.

She took off her shoes and lay on the bed.

For hours she had been in a state of tension but lying here, she felt her body ease a little. The plaster ceiling had a swirling pattern painted over many times.

She believed herself a coward. At the very least she lacked Charlie's conviction. He might be self-destructive, or driven by guilt, but he was still noble. She was too interested in her own story, too selfish, to sacrifice herself that way. Or perhaps other people's lives weren't real enough to her. Even if a cause was a good cause, that didn't mean it belonged to her. Or did one have to make it belong, make oneself belong? She didn't even know if she was running to something or away from something.

"I'm sorry," she said aloud, not knowing to whom she was speaking. She felt herself grow drowsy and closed her eyes.

She woke not with a start, but gradually, taking in the room. She hadn't turned on the light but it wasn't truly dark, not with the curtains open. She sat up and put her shoes back on. Then she picked up her case, locked the door behind her, and walked down the three flights of stairs to the lobby.

The young man looked up from his book.

"May I use the telephone?"

"There's a pay phone at the end of the ground floor hall."

"Can you make change for me?"

She carried her case down the hall but left it outside the folding door of the telephone booth as there wasn't enough room. She dialed the number of the house on Heddington. It was the number she had known since she was a little girl and that she was sure she would still remember when she was an old woman and had forgotten even her own name. She listened to the ring.

"Hello?" A male voice.

"Who is that?"

"Miriam? Thank God it's you. It's Andrei. Andrei Unterman."

"I only know one Andrei." Even now she couldn't help using that tone with him. "What are you doing there? It's past midnight."

"Your parents called me. They're worried sick. You have no idea what's going on here. They called the police. Now your father has gone to see Isidore in case he knows something. Are you all right?"

"Yes, I'm all right."

"Where are you?"

"At a hotel in Detroit."

"Detroit? What are you doing there?"

"I was going away. I can't explain now but I've changed my mind, I want to come home."

"Your father will come and get you."

"No, don't let him. I can't face him right now. Can you come?"

"Of course. But I have to let them know. Tell me exactly where you are."

§

Miriam sat in the dark, in the room in the Hotel Ross, her coat draped over her lap and her overnight case at her feet. She had turned on only the lamp on the night table and she read her book to the sound of the ticking clock. She found her pen and made a comment in the margin.

At three thirty a.m. she picked up the case, locked the door behind her, and took the stairs down to the lobby. The same young man was there, and he looked to be on the last page of his own book. He didn't look up until he reached the end and slowly turned it over.

"Can I help you with something?" he asked.

"I've changed my mind. I'm not staying. Someone is coming to pick me up."

"I'm not allowed to give your money back."

"That's all right. I'm going to wait down here, if you don't mind."

"Of course."

"Was your book good?"

"It was really good."

"What was it about?"

The young man scratched his chin. "It's about these three men who get off a train in some town in Texas. One of them looks kind of like a teacher, one is fat and sloppy, and one is just ordinary. It's July and scorching hot. I mean so that you're sweating even when you're just standing still. They take a taxi to the one hotel and that's when the author introduces the first of the people who live in the town, the driver. Because the book, you see, is as much about the people in the town as it is about the three strangers. And then the three strangers go up to their hotel room and start arguing and pretty soon you find out they've come to rob the bank. But right away you're not so sure it's going to go too well for them. But as I say, it's a way of showing all the life and the secrets of the town."

Miriam listened to the young man continue to describe the book. He didn't know, she thought, how to abbreviate a story. Of course it wasn't a book that she herself would read but it interested her that he could feel so excited about it, and it made her think that perhaps she was wrongly dismissive of this sort of thing and that perhaps there was more in it than she imagined. And then she realized that she was glad to have it to think about, rather than what she was doing, or what her parents would say, or what would happen next.

The house telephone rang and the young man answered it. "Somebody in 4B wants ice," he said. He went into the back office and came out again with a plastic bucket and went to the stairs. She walked to the front window and saw that it must have rained here, too — perhaps while she had slept, for the street glistened. And as she was looking out a car drove up slowly and bumped into the curb and stopped.

It was her father's car but the dark profile behind the wheel wasn't her father. It was Andrei. Somehow Andrei had convinced her father to let him drive all the way to Detroit and get her. She picked up her case and went out the door and down the steps.

She opened the back door and put in her case. She opened the passenger door and before she sat down she saw an apple resting on the seat. Andrei had brought her an apple. That was a very kind thing to do.

2005

SUNDAY, AUGUST 21

"I need your opinion, Mom. Come out to the garden."

As usual with Sharon, it was a command rather than a request. "You don't even like my taste," Miriam said as she followed her into the living room to the sliding door. The door stuck as usual but as she went through she put her hand tenderly on the glass.

"It's the florist," Sharon said. "I think the chuppah looks skimpy. But she says it's fine and that anyway it's too late. Whoever heard of a florist who didn't want to sell you more flowers?"

"I thought we'd decided already," Miriam said, meaning that Sharon had decided. Sharon brusquely waved her on; was it just mean to be annoyed by one's own daughter? The garden was small and almost square, with a profusion of roses blooming against the patched wooden fence and a red maple, one of the neighbourhood's oldest, rising massively from the corner to shade a good part of the lawn. There had been a freak storm on Friday, flooding streets and basements, causing car accidents and flight delays. Sharon had called her every hour, practically weeping about the imminent disaster. "It's not even your wedding, sweetheart," Miriam had said. "Michael's perfectly calm about it." They had cleaned up the debris and the flowers had miraculously sprung back. And here the day was warm, the remaining clouds scudding past the sun. The rented chairs had clacked open and now were lined in rows, their legs sinking a little into the spongy grass. The chuppah really was lovely, with its four driftwood posts (found up at the cottage) and the canopy made from quilted squares contributed by Michael and Miguel's friends. The squares were festooned with hearts and little embroidered birds, lines from popular songs, with sewn-on seashells and ceramic stars. It was Miriam, so notoriously incompetent in the traditional feminine arts, who had sewn them all together.

Some sort of vine wound up the posts, with sprays of small white flowers and every so often a lily. "Oh, it's just lovely," Miriam said and the florist with spikey orange hair turned and smiled at her. She wished in her own day there had been weddings like this, rather than the synagogue and banquet hall, the hair salon and the wedding gown and the registering. God, it had all been so stiff, she never thought to look at the photographs. And yet now it did come back to her, not the formality but the joy she had felt, how happy and sure. Now there was a fucking irony.

"What's a fucking irony?" Sharon stared at her. Had she really said that out loud? Maybe she was losing her mind. But no, she was just angry and sad. Much better to be angry. She turned her thoughts to Michael, who was getting married, and a desire to cry came over her that she resisted by trying to smile at Sharon's grim face.

"You never side with me, Mom. Not even against a stranger."

"I'm not trying to side with anyone."

"That's what you always say."

Well, it was Michael's wedding but without a doubt it was Sharon's affair. Not that she hadn't always liked to boss around her siblings, but the work she'd put into it — what exactly was she displacing? Her marriage seemed all right and the kids were great. But it had always seemed like a mistake for Sharon to give up her career, she'd liked it at Foreign Affairs. Perhaps Michael had agreed to let her organize out of feeling that she needed it, he was sensitive that way. If only Miriam could think of something to say to make it better.

"You've just done such a great job, Sharon."

"Whatever, Mom."

As if to save the day, Mia and Jeremy came racing up the aisle. Jeremy scooted past her to hide behind his broad-hipped mother. Laughing diabolically, Mia lunged at him from one side and then another.

"Enough," Sharon said. "I don't want you two getting all crazy. Your father's supposed to be watching over you."

"He's watching baseball instead," Jeremy said.

Sharon put a hand on each head as if to bestow a blessing, or perhaps anesthetize them. Either way, Miriam thought, it made a lovely picture. She said, "Did you two get to taste any desserts?"

"They're so yummy, you won't believe it."

"No more sugar. You'll go through the roof. By the way, Mom, when's Dad getting home?"

"He had an emergency consult. Your guess is as good as mine." She felt her face grow warm and half turned away, as if to examine the roses. "Speaking of missing people, where's our Ivy?"

"That girl is always hiding somewhere," Sharon said. "I didn't even know the desserts had arrived. Why didn't anyone tell me the caterers are here?"

§

She went looking for her granddaughter.

When Ivy was small, her favourite place was the space under the stairs. Miriam kept a flashlight there for her and Ivy would take in a stack of Archie comics. She would leave her for a while and then knock softly on the door and slide in a plate of cookies. Ivy got quite sad when she realized that she was growing too big to fit comfortably anymore. Everyone said she looked like Miriam in old photographs and that she had her stubbornness and powers of concentration and slight air of haughtiness, as if she had been secretly born of royalty. Of course the comparisons pleased Miriam, who thought Ivy too fiercely herself to resemble anyone. They were close because Ivy was the oldest and had spent the most time alone with her. Only lately had Jeremy started to come to lunch, and he was far less enthusiastic.

Ivy wasn't in the den or the downstairs washroom, so she went upstairs and looked into the bedrooms. The grooms' suits — not matching but complementary — were laid out on Michael's old bed, along with shirts, ties, boxers and shoes. The light blue suit had to be Miguel's; Michael would never have worn it.

She closed the door silently, as if afraid to disturb the clothing. The narrow stairway to the third floor was inside the walk-in linen closet. All these years she'd had the luxury of possessing the third floor for her study.

When they had bought it, the place had been a former rooming house — soiled carpets nailed to the floors, thin walls cutting up rooms, bathrooms like outhouses. She had agreed to take charge of the renovation even though she was three months pregnant and teaching a full load. But only if the third floor is mine, she had said. Well, he worked long hours and didn't need it anyway.

She came up through the trap door in the floor, into the dim and dusty light that was so quieting for her. She'd had bookshelves built against the walls, up to where they slanted with the roof, and her own three titles were on a bottom shelf next to a stack of journals. There were two simple worktables across from one another, and she went to the closest, a small stack of books at one end and at the other a single small book with a red cover that she had left there yesterday.

The Ambassadors. The same copy she had bought at Britnell's so long ago, the shop closed for half a dozen years now. She had taken it on the bus ride to Detroit but hadn't finished reading it until the following year in Paris. Almost every page was marked up, the margins filled, words underlined and circled, questions spelled out in block letters. Just the first three words of the novel — "Strether's first question" — had instigated a page of commentary on the facing blank.

She'd carried it everywhere in Paris, and brought it home, and kept it all this time, never writing about it, or

James, but not forgetting either, always knowing where it was. And why did now seem the right time, after forty-five or forty-six years, to take it down and read what she had written?

Because three days ago she had found out that her husband was having an affair again. And what had overwhelmed her first was not heartbreak but shame. As if she herself had done wrong.

But it wasn't for him, it was for herself that she came up here and found the book and stayed up for hours to decipher every word of marginalia in her young, minuscule handwriting. It had been familiar and strange, embarrassing and exhilarating, and she had wondered what the young person who had written all these words had to do with the old woman who read them now. And something had stirred in her, an idea — well, almost an idea — that gave her something else, something better, to think about.

It wasn't like anything she had written before and it scared her a little so that her impulse was to read new books and reread old ones in order to temporarily surround herself with other people's ideas. The books were in three piles on the opposite table, pushed together to make a wall, a protective wall, and she crossed over to them now. Recent works of queer theory that had upended thinking about Henry James: Jacobson and Stevens and Person and Bradley and Pigeon. But also theory and feminist texts to help clarify her own thoughts: Cixous, Kristeva, Heilbrun,

Sedgwick. And the latest Judith Butler, laying open and with a passage marked —

When the 'I' seeks to give an account of itself, it can start with itself, but it will find this self is already implicated in a social temporality that exceeds its own capacities for narration...

"Hey, Granny Minnie."

She started, pressing her palm to her heart. And there in the corner was Ivy, sitting in the reading chair by the window, not bothering to look up from her book. She wore a pretty yellow dress, her knees pulled up.

"I should have known to check my favourite place."

Ivy looked up now. Her eyesight was already poor and she picked up her glasses from the side table. "Can this space be mine, too? When I visit, I mean. You're so lucky."

"I am lucky, aren't I? But I think I could take in a partner."

"Good."

"What are you reading?"

"Oh, just absolute junk."

Her imitation of Sharon made Miriam laugh. "Yes, but what junk?"

She held the cover towards Miriam. *The Sisterhood of the Traveling Pants.*

"That's a funny name for a book."

"Well I read *The Half-Blood Prince* in three days and it was *so* dark and *so* tragic that I just needed something to lighten things up, you know? And a bunch of my friends — okay, they used to be my friends and they aren't anymore — but anyway they were passing it around and Julie, she asked if I wanted to read it which is the first time she's talked to me in a month so I thought it wouldn't be too smart to say no. It's about this girl who finds a pair of jeans in a thrift shop that turns out to somehow fit all her best friends even though they're not even the same size. It's the beginning of summer and they're all going someplace else but they make a promise to each wear the jeans and then send it to the next person and describe all their adventures while wearing them. I mean, it's a pretty stupid idea, like that would ever happen, and the girls are way too nice to each other, which in my opinion is less believable than *anything* in Harry Potter. But you know what? I can't put it down."

"It sounds quite delicious. I wonder what makes us just have to keep reading a book? Does that mean it's good and we don't want to admit it because it doesn't fit our idea of real literature? Or is it like eating candy? You know, all immediate pleasure but no nutrition."

"Mm," Ivy said, already lowering her head to read again.

Miriam went over to kiss her.

"Okay, Granny Minnie."

"Don't read through the wedding, now."

"I wouldn't. It's *Michael's* wedding."

This was a girl to warm a grandmother's heart. "Yes, it is."

"If you see Jeremy and Mia, don't tell them where I am."

Miriam winked at her. Her own father had liked to give a wink when she was little. She took a last look at Ivy, winding a few strands of hair around her finger as she read, and went back down the stairs.

§

There had always been something different about Michael, even when he was small. He was the sweetest boy, wanting to help her in the kitchen, worrying about his father's birthday, becoming deeply upset when they argued. And then as he got older he became secretive in a way she couldn't put her finger on. It was as if some thought would light up inside him and he would almost speak but then change his mind.

And then she just knew. There was no big revelation, no clue left in his trouser pockets (although she checked them), just an accumulation of small revelations. It was boys he liked. And for a time after that, she thought it explained everything about him.

When he was seventeen there was his first boyfriend, at least as far as she knew, someone older, someone who made him excited and happy and troubled and despairing and whose name he would never say. And the misery that followed. He locked himself in his room or didn't come home for hours — this went on for how long? Ten days at least. And then on a weekend, a Sunday she remembered because his father was at a conference in Los Angeles, she insisted that Michael have lunch in the garden with her. His sisters were conveniently elsewhere, Sharon at her part-time job and Hannah off somewhere with her pack of friends. She picked up a quiche from the Harbord Bakery and surprised him by pouring them both a glass of wine.

"You do know that people will love you for who you are."

"Please, Mom, let's not."

"Part of growing up is having your heart broken."

"I mean it, if you keep talking I'll get up."

"I know what a good person you are, Michael. So many good things are going to happen for you."

"Can we stop now?"

"Yes, we can stop. Eat. You've lost weight. And the quiche is quite good."

It wasn't as if everything got better after that, but he did slowly return to himself. That was before anyone had heard of AIDS and, when it came, thank God he was so naturally restrained, though he would have been angry at her if she'd said that. Those friends of his who had become ill, and he'd helped to take care of—how awful that was. Possibly it had changed him, possibly it just made him more like the Michael she knew.

And then he found Miguel. Who was so different from Michael, a naturally happy disposition, a little flamboyant, outwardly affectionate. So exactly the man that Michael needed. That was seven years ago and now they were getting towards forty. Miguel, whose hairline was already receding, shaved his head. Michael had appealing lines around his eyes. It was the loveliest story and for today it was all she needed.

§

She was on the stairs when her cellphone rang. Where had she left it? On the old dresser that stood by the front door. The big drawers stuck and while the kids were growing up there were always scarves and sweaters hanging out. Hurrying down, she just missed colliding with a man in a waiter's uniform carrying a tray of champagne glasses. She grabbed the phone and flipped it open.

"Mir? I'm sorry but I'm going to be another little while. There's been a bit of a fuck-up in surgery."

She didn't say anything.

"Miriam, are you there?"

"I'm here."

"Really, I'm sorry. This is terrible timing. I don't mean just the surgery, I mean everything. I'm sorry you had to find out—"

"That's why you're sorry?"

"No, it didn't come out right. You know we can get through this, like we did before."

"That was years ago."

"Exactly. Everything's been good until now. Nothing has to change. Just give me a moment to work things out."

"I think it's me that has to work things out. Maybe I should go away for a while."

"Where would you go?"

How could she know, when she'd just thought of it? "You're about to miss Michael's wedding."

"He's my son, too, you know. I've made it clear that I'm out of here in a half hour, no matter what."

"Then I don't know why you're phoning me. Call Sharon. She's the one who's worried."

"Jesus, Miriam, is this the way it's going to be? We really need to talk."

She shut her eyes. "I'll see you when you get here." Slowly she shut the phone. She went to the front door and looked at the stained-glass oval window. It showed a forest of evergreens and a little cabin in the distance. All the children had been fascinated by that cabin, speculating about where it might be and who might live in it. One day

Hannah had declared it the home of the three bears and so it had been ever since.

A premonition came to her, as if there had been a slight change in air pressure or a vibration under her feet. She opened the door.

Brunswick Avenue. The day was warming and the earlier rain had brought out the scent of the rhododendrons lining the path. Sparrows flitted, making a racket. On the other side of the street a man with a limp was putting something through the mail slot of the opposite house. Not the postman, it was Sunday, just flyers for pizza delivery and real estate agents.

A couple of racing bikes went by, the men in Spandex looking ridiculous. She walked to the curb and looked up towards Bloor Street where people were crossing the road, then looked south where it was quiet. She felt the premonition again and a second later saw an airport cab turn onto the street. It came up slowly and stopped at the curb. She couldn't see through the tinted windows and had to wait to see her youngest, Hannah, backing out of the passenger seat, hauling behind her an enormous backpack. She'd done something to her hair. It was boy-short and streaked with red.

"Hey, Mom!"

She came skipping up to throw her slim arms around Miriam's neck. Hannah, always the most demonstrative, needing signs of love.

"You must be so beat, sweetheart. Are you okay?"

"God, what a long trip! I don't even know what day it is anymore. And I've never felt so grungy in my life. It's so weird to be back. How are the preparations going?"

"Your sister has everything well in hand."

"Do I have to salute the sergeant major?"

"Don't start. She's doing a great job. And everyone's going to be so glad to see you. Eight months and three weeks and two days."

"Seriously, you've counted? Always the mom. Are the boys here yet? And where's Dad?"

"The boys are supposed to stay away a little longer. The timing's very exact. Meanwhile, your father is stuck at the hospital."

"I thought he was cutting back, especially now that you're retired."

"I hate that word. You're actually here, let me hold you again. Oh, you really do need a wash. Go inside and let everybody see you. I'll be there in a minute."

She watched Hannah drag her backpack into the house and then stood by herself a moment, feeling the presence of her three children in the same city.

§

In the wainscoted dining room, Sharon and Hannah were already having an argument. They had the same body language as when they were kids — Sharon leaning forward, one hand on her hip, gesturing; Hannah back on her heels, both hands up, face half turned.

"Give me a break," said Hannah. "How could I prepare if I didn't get the email?"

"Didn't get it or didn't open it? I don't know why I bother to even say anything. It's never worked before."

"Well, you're not my mother. *She's* my mother."

"Yes," Miriam said, "and this is not the time for whatever you two are doing."

Hannah turned huffily away. "I'm going to take a shower."

"There's at least three other people who need showers, too," Sharon said.

"Yes, but they didn't come from fucking Australia. Good to see you, too, sis."

And she dragged her pack up the stairs, letting it thump on each step.

"I didn't mean for that to happen," Sharon said. "But she is absolutely no help."

"You need to make it up when she comes down."

"I've got too many other things to worry about. Now I need to find someone to go on an errand."

"What errand?"

"It turns out that two people need lactose-free milk. As if they couldn't just have their coffee black."

"Let me go for it. I could use a little walk. Unless there's something else you want me to do."

"No, go. It's one less thing for me to have to worry about. But don't be long."

Sharon walked briskly towards the kitchen. Of course it was Sharon and not Hannah who would brood over their spat. And now where had she put her purse? Not hanging from the radiator in the hall where she usually left it. She hoped this was normal, forgetting where one put things or the names of people one hadn't seen for a while. Seventy wasn't really old, not the way she'd thought of it when she was young, but it was something. And there was her purse up on the hat shelf, a woven bag she'd bought in Mexico last year. When everything had still been all right, unless Miriam had been deluded.

She went out. Across Bloor Street was the falafel restaurant where Sharon had lasted a week in her first job. They used to imitate what the owner had said when he fired her: *A vaitress has to be villing to take orders.* So many sayings they used to share, references and in-jokes only their family could get. Now the children were grown up and it had all faded away. But that was supposed to happen, that was just the passing of time.

Three Chinese women in slippers passed her, each carrying stuffed Honest Ed's bags. She passed the South American gift shop, the used CD store, the framing place that was overpriced but did a good job. Further ahead someone with an accordion was playing Dylan in front of the Brunswick House. She paused in front of Book City. It was hardly her idea of a lovely old bookshop, not with its linoleum floor and metal shelves and pharmacy-bright lighting. But the selection of books was good and she hadn't been in for at least a couple of weeks; surely a couple of minutes wouldn't hurt.

On the front table she looked at the new titles stacked up. *Never Let Me Go. On Beauty. Runaway. A Field Guide to Getting Lost.* She brushed her fingers lightly over their covers.

"Professor Moscowitz?"

A young woman was smiling at her, oval face and almond eyes and heavy dark hair, pulling away her earbuds. "I took your Woolf seminar."

"Enaya. How nice. I'm trying to remember where you went off to."

"Yale."

"That's right. And you're happy there?"

She wrinkled up her face. "It's complicated."

Miriam nodded and they spontaneously laughed together. "Graduate school is to be endured as much as anything else. Really, I shouldn't be in here, I've been sent to get some milk. If you want to walk with me—"

"Yes, sure. I'm in town for the summer staying with friends. But they're busy today and I'm just wandering."

They left the store and continued down Bloor. She was trying to remember if Enaya was from Iran or Egypt or possibly Jordan. She did recall that her parents were some sort of professionals — engineers maybe — and that they called almost every day wanting to know what she did and who she spent her time with. And the girl herself had some notable neuroses about illnesses and deadlines.

"And how's your family?"

"Everyone is well. They would be very disappointed if I ended up back there. I have to start job hunting soon. Or a post-doc at least."

"That's so stressful."

"I have this fear that I'll get only one offer and it'll be at some little college in Arkansas and I'll be the only Muslim."

"Now I know what's different. You used to wear a hijab."

"I took it off about a year ago. But I still practise."

They reached the Dominion and went through the turnstile, heading to the dairy section. Miriam had never bought lactose-free milk and had to look closely at the label. They went to the cashier and then onto the street again.

"My son is getting married today," Miriam said.

"Oh, my goodness. And here you are talking to me! I didn't mean to take up your time."

"No, it's fine. My daughter is in complete charge. I'm just the host. You don't have anything to do this afternoon. Why not come?"

"Oh, I couldn't! That is a crazy idea."

"I want you to. But maybe I should mention that my son is gay and he's marrying a man. In case that makes a difference."

"And it's legal in this country?"

"For a month now. And it's been recognized by the province for two years."

"I had no idea. Yes, I'd love to come but only if you mean it. Oh, but I don't have the right clothes."

"You look fine. Listen, I'm sure we have a few minutes. Want to have a coffee with me?"

"Of course, if you really have time."

They were standing in front of Dooney's. Miriam held the door for them and then sat at a marble-topped table. The burly, soft-voiced owner came around from the bar.

"I'll have an espresso," Miriam said.

"Peppermint tea, please."

"Tell me about your thesis. I miss students like you, just as much as I thought I would."

"Really? Your thoughts would be so valuable to me. Because I am very insecure and my advisor is not being as helpful as I had hoped. I have an abstract in my bag. But you don't want to read it now—"

"Of course I do, hand it over."

Enaya fished in her bag and came up with the sheet. The espresso was set down beside her and Miriam raised the cup as she read. *Individualism, Nationalism, and Gender in the Postcolonial Arabic Novel.*

"You've got a draft done?"

"All but the last two chapters."

"I won't know your primary texts. But still, if you'd like me to read it."

"That would be so generous —"

"Can you bring it by the house tomorrow? I've just had this thought of going away and if I do I would need to take it with me."

"Of course I will. But what a shame you're going away. We have a little study group for the summer. I would have invited you to visit with us. But of course you would have been too busy anyway."

"No, I would have been glad to come. The truth is I wasn't sure that I wanted to retire. But my husband wanted us to slow down, not that he has at all. Anyway, I thought the university could use someone new."

"I don't know about that. But where are you going?"

"I don't know. Have you got any ideas for me?" Miriam laughed.

"My parents in Amman would be very happy to let you have their guest house."

"That would certainly be an adventure." She took a bill from her wallet and put it down. "No, leave your purse alone, please. We better walk straight back. My daughter will be having just a little fit about now. Now don't forget to bring me your draft."

"Thank you so, so much, Professor Moscowitz."

"Call me Miriam."

"Miriam. And will you tell me what you are working on?"

Miriam shrugged. "It's just an idea. I'm not really sure it's anything at all."

"Yes?"

"Henry James."

"And?"

"Well, and me. But look at the time. We better get back to the house. I'm very glad you're coming, Enaya."

§

She had managed to complete her undergraduate degree and then had gone to Paris in August 1958. Her father had been against it; it was her mother who, seeing the depressed condition she was in, quietly persuaded him to at least pay for her airplane ticket. She had found an inexpensive apartment on Rue Tournefort, a former maid's room on the top floor of an apartment house. She found a part-time job in the office of a fabric distributor with overseas clients and took courses at the Sorbonne. Her written and spoken French improved remarkably. Once a week she wrote a long letter to Andrei Unterman, trying to amuse but also telling him about her state of mind and the progress of her thought. This writing, on laid paper with a new fountain pen, she performed on her free Friday afternoons at a small café near the university, and it became an important point in the week for her. Andrei had begun to work for a small Jewish law firm. His letters in return were considerably shorter but he appraised her ideas seriously.

Did her letters still exist? It was a long time ago, there was no reason they ought to, not with Andrei moving so many times in those days and then finally settling in Calgary. The sorry fact was that she had long ago lost his.

In Paris she began to dream in French. She might have stayed longer but for the acceptance, with scholarship, from Radcliffe. Radcliffe had been a very different experience from the University of Toronto. She had lived in Holmes Hall with her own key so she could come and go as she pleased. All the graduate courses at Harvard were available to her. She went to the theatre, to poetry readings at Club Passim, and she was invited to soirées at the Cambridge houses of her professors.

She stayed in the United States, getting her first job at a college in Connecticut. But after five years her father began to experience heart trouble and she wanted to come back. And really, for better or worse, she felt that she belonged in the city and would always be a foreigner anywhere else. And then a position in the English department of University College became available.

She got the job and came home. She would never forget the day she moved into an office beneath the arches, just as she had dreamed as an undergraduate. By then the college library had been built, closing in the garden quad. And Professor Birmingham had retired. But he made an appearance at the faculty Christmas party, his beard gone white, face yellowish and gaunt. He used a cane but still had presence. She wanted to say: *You couldn't keep me out, after all.* Or just kick the cane out from under him. When she approached he smiled — in recognition? But then he turned to give the same smile to someone else.

And now she, too, had given up her office for someone younger, someone up-to-date. It gave her a rare moment of sympathy for Birmingham, dead these many years.

§

As they reached the house a van pulled up to the curb. A man and woman in white jumped out, went round the back, and slid out large trays wrapped in cellophane.

"I thought the caterers were already here," Miriam said. "I guess they waited to bring the main course for fear of poisoning everyone."

Enaya said, "I heard about such a wedding."

"Really?"

"Food poisoning. The guests filled up the local hospitals. Later when they watched the video of the wedding, everyone yelled at the screen, "No! Don't eat the salmon!"

"Oh God, that's awful. Not to mention, we're having salmon. You can eat that, right?"

"But there won't be a meal prepared for me. I don't mind, I'm never hungry."

"Trust me, they always bring a few extras. Let's go in."

"You are really sure?"

Miriam took her arm. They let the catering people pass back out the door before they went in. There was a distinctly higher level of bustle than when she had left. People she didn't recognize were moving purposefully through the first floor. And here were her two nephews, young men in their twenties, looking uncomfortable in their suits by the fireplace that had never worked.

"Hey, Auntie Miriam." The younger one, Solomon, came over and kissed her. His brother Daniel had something in his mouth and just nodded.

"It's so good to see you both. Daniel, you look more like your father all the time."

"Ah, don't tell me that!"

"This is my friend, Enaya. She isn't going to know anyone at the wedding."

"You know us, don't you?" Solomon said. "Dad made us come early for some reason and now we're just in the way. You can be in the way with us."

"That sounds like a good invitation," said Enaya.

She left them talking and went looking for her brother, glad for all the people who would be filling the house. She hadn't seen Brian for six months as she herself had taken advantage of his visits to see their mother by going to the cottage. The boys were from his first marriage and there had been some estrangement between father and sons after the divorce. But they liked his second wife, who was so much easier to talk to than Brian himself and seemed to make him less intense, too.

And there was Brian looking out the back door with a small dog on a leash. He wore a black suit, the same that he'd been wearing at such events for years, and he needed a haircut, so tufts of steely hair stood up above his ears.

"I can't believe you brought the dog."

He turned and gave his enigmatic smile. "Our dog sitter wasn't available. I'll shut him in a room upstairs. He's too slow to care these days."

She bent down to scratch the creature as it tried to lick her face. "Hey, Gus, how you doing?" To her brother she said, "I heard your plane got delayed by the rain. So you didn't get up to Mom's?"

"There wasn't time. When is she coming?"

"They're taking a cab. I told Jinette not to bring her early, she gets tired so quickly around people. Why are they moving the chairs?"

"The rabbi, or whoever she is, thought they needed more room for the ceremony."

She stood up again. "So are you leaving Bombardier?"

"I went in to tell them and they promoted me. You look tired, Minnie. Is everything okay?"

She put her hand on his arm. "So, brother, here's a question. If you were thinking of going away for a while, where would you go?"

"Go away? With Zev?"

"By myself."

He looked hard at her, but she just put on an expression of curious interest.

"Hmm, where would I go? I'd like to visit the Smithsonian again."

"That's not what I mean."

"Okay, okay. I'd go to Frobisher Bay. No, Iqaluit it's called now. I'd love to see the Arctic."

She pursed her lips. "Nice idea. By the way, where's Victoria?"

"Nosing around the kitchen, I think."

Someone called, "Mom!" from above and she stepped into the backyard and turned around to look up at the house. Sharon was leaning out an upstairs window. "Oh hi, Uncle Brian. Mom, can you come up here? We're having a little crisis."

"What sort of crisis?"

"Just get up here."

She gave her brother a look that made him chuckle. Then she went back into the house and up the stairs. Sharon was in her old bedroom, used now as a guest room for visiting friends or nomadic young people befriended by Hannah on her travels. She knocked gently before going in to see Sharon standing with her hands on her hips and pointing to Mia, or rather to her one pudgy leg sticking out from under the bed. Jeremy sat in the desk chair playing with some action figures.

"Hmm. What's up?"

Sharon pretended to strangle herself. "Mia has decided she doesn't want to be the flower girl after all."

"No!" Mia cried from under the bed. She kicked her leg feebly.

"But you were so excited about it yesterday."

"I can be the flower girl," Jeremy said.

"You're already the ring boy and that's pretty big," Sharon said.

Miriam crouched down so Mia could hear her better. "I say, if you're not going to do it I'll have to give the job to someone else who I know won't do it as well as you. But first, can I at least see the dress we chose? I can't remember what colour it is. Is it green?"

"It's lavender." She said *lavember*.

"Oh, I don't think so."

Mia wiggled out from under the bed. She stood up and brushed her skirt with her hands. "See?"

"You're right. It *is* lavender. Remember how much fun we had picking it out? Oh, well. I'll go down and find another girl. I'm sure Ivy would say yes, she's done it before."

"No."

"You don't want another girl to do it?"

"No."

"So will you do it?"

"No!"

But this struck Mia as funny and she leaned back her head and laughed.

"You really are a goose. So will you do it?"

"No!"

She laughed louder. A thundering of feet in the hall and a moment later Hannah threw open the door.

"They're here!"

§

The heart leaps. There was no other expression.

Miriam joined the crowd pushing its way to the front door and onto the porch. She would have cried, *Out of the way, I'm the mother*, if it wouldn't have made her ridiculous. Everyone was talking excitedly, Sharon and Hannah were at the porch rail, Brian had a video camera in one hand and the dog under the other arm, her nephew Solomon was saying something into Enaya's ear. Even Ivy came out and pulled herself up onto the brick pedestal that held up one of the wooden porch pillars.

And there were Michael and Miguel. On matching bicycles. Michael with his shy, quietly happy face and

Miguel showing his beautiful teeth like a movie star. People streamed off the porch to greet them.

She felt a small hand in hers and looked down to see Mia.

"Do you want to come with me to say hi?"

Mia nodded. So they went down, and waited their turn, though Michael kept glancing at Miriam, his eyes bright. First they reached Miguel, who lifted Mia in a hug and then kissed Miriam on each cheek.

"Now you will be my mother."

Miriam blushing. "And you'll always be the man who made my Michael happy."

"Not an easy job!" Miguel said and laughed. And then Miriam turned to Michael, who was crouching down and talking seriously to Mia. Mia nodded solemnly and looked up at Miriam and Miriam smiled at her.

"Mom." And her son was enveloping his small mother. And she feeling his warmth.

A sharp clap of hands. "Excuse me!" Sharon announced. "This is all very nice but the guests are going to start arriving in less than an hour and we're not ready."

They began filing back inside, all but Miriam who lingered by the rail. She listened to the slight rustle of the leaves overhead. So little had changed on the street. She remembered standing here and watching Sharon learning to ride a bike, her father trotting beside her, promising that he would keep ahold of the seat and then gently letting go.

And as Sharon rode slowly on her own, unaware that she was free, he turned and flashed Miriam a smile that said, *See, isn't our daughter amazing? Aren't I a wonderful dad? Don't you love me?* And all of those things had been true.

§

On the oak sideboard were laid the sets of cutlery rolled in napkins, the glasses and buckets of ice. The sideboard had come from her parent's house on Heddington; she remembered how her mother had lovingly polished its shining surface. Now a person couldn't give one away. She was counting the cutlery on order from Sharon when the musicians arrived, two men and a woman in black carrying violin, viola, and cello in their cases.

Her cellphone rang; she didn't remember slipping it into her pocket. The number was from her mother's room.

"Mom?"

"It's me, Jinette. Your mother wouldn't get in the cab. I had to send him away. She's getting so stubborn."

"Okay, okay. I'll be there straightaway. Try to be downstairs, that'll save us a few minutes."

"I'm sorry."

"Don't be, you're an angel. See you soon."

She found her keys in the lopsided bowl that Hannah had made in pottery class. Sharon spied her at the door.

"You're not even dressed. Where are you going?"

"Bubby won't get in a cab."

"Oh shit. There isn't much time."

"Well, we can't start without her. I'll be back in a jiffy."

She should have planned to pick up her mother in the first place. Probably it was an act of avoidance; even now, in her condition, her mother was difficult and judgmental. Why did fathers and daughters have a so much simpler relationship? It had been just as true in their own house; the girls had always been harder on her than Zev.

The Volvo was parked in the drive and she got in and quickly backed into the street. On Sunday the traffic was light. As she drove she felt a surge of longing for her father. A man who put on a tie every morning, even after retiring. Who would examine the children's feet, pronounce them the most perfect he had ever seen, and then tickle them into hysterics. Who continued to take the occasional Sunday walk with her and then go for tea, complaining that the old restaurants had been replaced by chain cafes. He had spent a lot of time with Michael, "grandson number one," taking him to the park, then movies, and every week for swimming lessons followed by corn beef sandwiches at one of the remaining delicatessens. Later when she had tried to ease him into understanding Michael's homosexuality, her father had refused to listen, but she believed he would have accepted it in time. He would have been so happy today, she was sure of it.

At Eglinton Avenue traffic slowed. There were always old Jewish people driving here, so shrunken they could barely see over the dashboard. At last she turned into the Baycrest driveway and there, good as always, was Jinette standing behind her mother in the wheelchair.

She got out and opened the back door. "Mom, you look beautiful. I love that dress we chose. And Jinette did such a nice job on your hair."

Her mother smiled like the queen. Jinette said, "We had a good time getting ready, didn't we?" She wore a simple cotton dress and plastic sandals. Her hair had been done in those tight cornrows that took so many hours.

"You forgot my birthday," said her mother.

"No, Mom, it's Michael's wedding."

"I know. He's a wonderful boy. Visits me all the time."

Meaning, Miriam was sure, that she was a bad daughter. She came twice a week, wheeled her mother to the park in good weather, brought her home for Friday night dinners. "We have to hurry just a little. Let me help you get into the car."

"Jinette can help me."

"That's fine."

Miriam struggled to fold up the wheelchair and get it into the trunk. Jinette buckled her mother into the back seat and got into the passenger side.

"You're a godsend, Jinette."

"She's a little confused today. But she's so apprecia-
tive, more than I can say for my own family." She chuckled.
"And Michael's getting married. My, my."

"Tell me, Jinette, if you could go anywhere you
wanted tomorrow, where would you go."

"Now there's a question. I'd go to Kingston and see
all my aunties and uncles and nieces and nephews."

"You go to Jamaica every year."

"And where else would I want to go?"

"Are you going somewhere nice?" said her mother.

"That's a good question, Ma." Miriam stepped on
the gas.

§

When they had met, her first year back in Toronto, Zev was
doing his residency in thoracic surgery. It was at a dinner
party, which was the thing then, people showing off the
newly purchased house, and he was sitting across from
her and down so they didn't get to talk during the meal.
A full head of chestnut hair, warm brown eyes, a strong,
prominent nose, and he was clever and quick and deep-
voiced. He was attracting the attention of the women on
either side of him but every so often he would look at her.

After dinner he came up to her. She was holding a
drink in the living room while she pretended to look at a
painting. "So, is it speaking to you?" he asked. "To me it's

whispering how much it cost." They began to talk easily, she couldn't remember about what, only that she found it refreshing when he didn't give her his pedigree. It was only later from the hostess that she found out he was six years younger than her, a Westmount Montreal Jew, his father a doctor with a large reputation. He seemed more interested in talking about her, why she had come back, the work she was doing, whether she was impressed or disappointed by her students.

Much later she saw him do this to others, bring his full attention, as if no one could be more fascinating. But this sort of disillusionment always happened; a person wasn't as original, or thoughtful, or kind as they appeared in the first flush of attraction. And their first years had been good. He had supported her teaching when almost no mothers they knew went back to work. Even so, she had to give up a lot of her research and writing time, so two or three books never got written. But you didn't think about these things in the day-to-day, trying to keep it all going, and then the kids grew up and moved out and thirty-seven years of marriage went by.

This wasn't his first affair, of course she knew that. There had been one when the kids were young but he had stopped it as soon as she'd found out; he hated to be thought badly of and had begged her to forgive him. She'd had the kids to think of and, hurt though she was, she did not seem to feel as possessive as other women. The second (at least that she knew of) happened ten years later, and this time it alienated her so much — not only from him but also from herself — that she began her own affair with an instructor in the French department. The whole thing had disgusted her in a way that being unfaithful to Isidore never had, perhaps because she'd been so much younger, or because Charlie Kroken had meant something to her. But this affair had made her burn with shame and when the man had said that he was in love with her she had immediately broken it off.

But that too was long behind them. They'd somehow found one another again, if less completely, always holding a little of themselves back. The kids were gone and they both put in longer hours, he at the hospital and she with her courses and supervising more students and receiving invitations to lecture at other universities. And they'd been fine, enjoying each other's company, taking their annual trips to the Laurentians and to Europe, sharing a delight in their grandkids. At sixty-four he had a runner's slim frame, his face almost gaunt, his hair touched with silver. The charm remained, the easy, entitled air that doctors of his generation wore like an overcoat draped on the shoulders. She had suspected nothing — "suspect," what a word! — until she found the letter in his jacket pocket. Someone else might believe that Zev had wanted her to discover it but she knew that he felt invulnerable, which made him careless. Maybe her turning seventy had done something to him, had made him feel that she'd crossed some invisible line that he wasn't ready for.

Not wanting to face him, she'd phoned Zev at the hospital to say she knew. There was a long pause, as if he were considering various options, before he began to speak in measured tones. He was truly sorry, this had nothing to do with her nor did it affect the way he felt about her. If she would only be patient for a little while.

She did not want to be patient. But what did she feel now? Shame had given way to anger. She could have slapped him across the face. And hurt, of course. But mostly it felt as if her arms had been holding everything up, holding everything together without her even realizing it, and suddenly it was all too heavy and cumbersome and painful and she just wanted to let go so that everything could fall.

She ought to leave him. But she was seventy years old and knew what that meant. It meant she would spend the rest of her life alone. Waking up with no one beside her. Silence in every room. Dinners with only a book or a magazine or the television. No walking trips together. No shared memory of the kids when they were little, or of some funny incident in a restaurant. No occasional comforting sex. And when she became sick, or grew infirm — oh, it was all too miserable to think about.

§

She pulled the car into the drive and hurried round to get the wheelchair out of the trunk. Hannah came out, looking lithe in a loose tie-dyed dress and necklace of wooden beads. She kissed her grandmother on the cheek and helped her out of the back seat. "Bubby, I haven't seen you in ages. It's me, Hannah, your favourite! Isn't that what I always say? Everyone's waiting to see you."

"Are they?"

"Mom, you'd better get dressed before Sharon has a total meltdown. A few people have arrived early."

"Is your father here?"

"Not that I know."

"All right. Hannah, you'll help? And remember, Jinette, you're not just here to watch my mother. We'll all spend time with her. You're a guest, too."

"Don't you worry about that. I'm planning on enjoying myself."

"By the way, Mom," said Hannah, "is it okay if I stay at the house a while? Till I figure out a job and stuff."

"You don't have to ask. It's always your house, too."

Miriam ran inside and went straight up the stairs without catching anyone's eye. At least she'd had the foresight to shower and shave her legs this morning. She pulled off her clothes, rolled some deodorant under her arms, and wiggled into her dress, which felt a touch tighter than when she'd tried it on a month ago. At the dressing table she put a thin line around her eyes and picked up a lipstick.

A knock on the door.

"I have no privacy. So come on in, whoever it is."

In the mirror she watched the door slowly open and saw Andrei's uncertain face appear. With an intake of breath she rose to put her arms around him. "Aw, Andrei. I've been so hoping you would make it."

He was heavier in his dark suit, his face round and unlined. His remaining arc of hair was cut short, making his ears prominent. But the same kindly look in his eyes.

"What a day, Miriam. Just thinking about it has cheered me up all week."

"You're a sweetheart. Michael's always been so fond of you. It really is something, isn't it? And just seeing you." She put her hand on her heart. "The things we've gone through. When I see you — it brings so much back. I see my father at the dinner table. And Brian with his rocket ships. And me being so mean to you."

"You were just teasing. I was grateful for the attention."

"Oh, I was terrible!"

"Hey, I just saw your mother downstairs. She looks very well. And she recognized me. I was really touched."

"I'm not surprised she'd know you. And how is everything, Andrei? How is Suki?"

He shrugged. "She's well enough for me to leave for a day or two, so that's something. Of course she insisted. She really regrets not being here."

"I know. I'm just so, so sorry, Andrei. I'm going to come next week and tell her all about the wedding myself. Would that be all right?"

"She would love it. Bring photographs if you get any. Looking at photographs is her thing at the moment."

"I will. And the kids and grandkids?"

"They've been really good, coming to Calgary every chance they can. It's a close time for everyone. And I think Tamiko's going to come home and stay. But Miriam, I was sent upstairs by Sharon to give you a ten-minute warning. You're the hostess, you know. I didn't see Zev."

"He has a knack for getting to places in the nick of time. Riding in on his white steed. Oh, Andrei —"

He was the only one she had ever told about the previous affairs, and he had listened patiently without judgment or advice. But she couldn't do that to him now, really it was so trivial in comparison. Instead she said, "You're not carrying anything so I guess you don't still have the letters. I knew it was a long shot."

"You seriously underestimate me, Miriam." Smiling, he turned and, opening the door, reached down and picked up a flat box that had been left in the hall. He held it out to her."

"You *did* keep them?"

"Did you really have any doubt?"

"Thank you so much for bringing them." She took off the lid and saw the letters, carefully unfolded and flattened, their pages paperclipped, the envelopes in a rubber-banded pile on top. She could remember writing four or five but here were dozens and dozens of pages: thirty letters, fifty? She picked one up near the top.

First of all, I had no idea (because really I know nothing) that Paris shuts down in August. Shutters closed, locks locked, signs hung (Fermé pour vacances). The natives had decamped for the south and even the rental agencies were closed. But I found a notice on a bulletin board and managed to get a three-month sublet. The little room is stultifyingly hot and if I open the window cats come in at night. I keep a supply of shoes by my bed ready for tossing . . .

Putting it back, she drew out another.

So I decided to be bold. I asked each professor in my très charmant français if I might be allowed to observe and every one of them said yes and only one of them leered at me. So now I'm a regular and the administration seems at last willing to recognize my presence and sometimes I'm brave enough to ask a question. But I haven't got to the important stuff, which is how exciting the ideas are. Some of them come from Russians, some from French, and all of it is turning my thoughts upside down . . .

"Miriam?"

She looked up. "Oh God, of course. One second."

She put the lid back on the box, looked around the room and then leaned down to slip it under the bed. She pushed it farther in with her foot.

"We better run, Andrei. Come on."

She took his hand a moment and squeezed it. They went out of the room to the top of the stairs where she could hear the buzz of voices and laughter. She gave him a quick smile and then started down.

§

The guests were pouring into the house. She stood just past the vestibule, greeting people, getting kissed, making introductions, suggesting they move through to the back garden and take their seats.

Sharon appeared beside her. "You better take your place, Mom. I'll put a waiter on the door for any late-comers."

"What about your father?"

"He's already here."

So he had avoided looking for her and even though she didn't want to see him she was disappointed. She worked her way through the crowd, which seemed in no hurry to stop talking. Someone kissed her cheek, some-one whispered into her ear, someone touched her wrist.

Enaya said, "I've missed everything back home. All the weddings and births, even the funerals. You are so kind to invite me."

Solomon came up beside Enaya. "I've saved seats if you want to sit with us."

"How nice."

Some word had spread, for people now hurried to find seats. She let them pass and then followed, through the sliding door to the garden. The sun shone and there was just the slightest breeze ruffling the flowers. The trio of musicians was seated at the side and playing, the chairs were almost all full. By the trellised wall she saw the line-up for the procession. And there at last was Zev, looking at her with an expression upon which it was easy to impose her own interpretation — guilty, anxious, rueful, hard-hearted — handsome as always with his silver hair swept back and his blue eyes, the perfectly cut suit, the silk tie knotted exactly. He gave a public smile as she walked over to stand beside him.

"Miriam —"

"I just want to enjoy this. To take in every moment. That's all I want right now."

"Of course."

She turned to say a word to Miguel and his sister, a worn-looking woman of perhaps forty-five, his only family member to come. They had met at a restaurant last night for the first time but the poor woman, who had never been out of Venezuela and didn't speak English, had looked desperately uncomfortable the whole time.

And now Michael came to stand between her and Zev. Zev kissed him and in turn Michael kissed Miriam who immediately teared up.

"I'll stop, I promise," she said. "Are you nervous?"

"I feel sick, actually."

The music changed, becoming slow and stately, and the woman who was to officiate, a judge, began to walk down the aisle in her robe. Next came Jeremy holding the case with the rings, marching stiffly and looking straight ahead.

Mia waited her turn, her eyes large, the wicker basket of petals in her hand. Miriam leaned down to her. "Not too fast, sweetheart. Let everyone see your lovely smile."

She began to walk almost too slowly. "Throw the petals!" hissed Sharon and Mia put her fingers into the basket and came up with a clump of petals that she dropped all at once. Michael took in a breath. "Don't let me collapse," he said, and the three of them began to walk. People held out their hands or leaned into the aisle to kiss Michael. Behind them came Miguel and his sister. They reached the chuppah and stood under one side of it and then Michael and Miguel took a step towards one another.

§

Tinkling of glasses that started in one corner of the living room and spread. Miguel put his hands on Michael's shoulders to gently turn him, then kissed him lingeringly on the lips.

Hooting around the room. There was no formal seating so the speakers had merely stood up and raised their voices. First had been Sharon, then their friends Leon and Geoffrey and then Hannah. Miguel got half the room teary-eyed. Miriam had made it clear she wouldn't speak but Zev rose to give a portrait of Michael as a little boy — his watchfulness, his serious questions and silent consideration of the answers. He was always easy in front of an audience and she enjoyed watching him, at least until he began to say how proud *we* were of him, what a good son he was to *us,* how *we* were glad to have Miguel as part of *our* family. And then he looked her way and smiled, not for her but for the crowd.

He got down and she was glad for the last of the speeches. But then Michael rose and went to the microphone. Michael who hated public speaking. He pulled at his tie, cleared his throat, took a breath.

"My name is Michael and I'm the groom. Well, one of them." Scattered chuckles. "I know we've made a lot of toasts tonight already. And we're not trying to get you drunk. At least, I don't think so. There have been a lot of speakers already. I think the Pope might show up next."

Miguel shouted, "God forbid!"

"Hey, you've had your turn. Anyway. All I was going to do was get up here and say thank you for coming, I love you, and now please go home. As most of you know, I'm not crazy about speaking in pubic. But I can't do that because there is one person who hasn't come up here to say anything. My mother. Miriam."

Applause and whistles.

"Minnie to a select few. To be honest, I'm surprised, because Miriam is a fine public speaker. She lectured to eager students for about forty years. She has rarely lacked for words. Or opinions, for that matter. Opinions about the news of the day, or larger social or political ills, or just whether you should get a haircut. Nor has she lacked for causes. I see my sisters nodding. But honestly, my mother has always helped me to see that the world is a larger place than just the circle of our own lives. And that we are part of that larger world and have a responsibility to it.

"My mother isn't coming up because she says she'll just weep and make a fool of herself. Which is funny because I don't think my mother has ever worried about how she looks to other people. Anyway, even if she did come up here all she'd do is say nice things about Miguel. Maybe something about me. But I think it's time to say something about her.

"My mother was the first person in my family to realize that I was gay. I was a teenager and I hardly knew myself. This wasn't easy for her but not because of any prejudice. It was because she worried about the prejudice of others, about the ignorance and contempt and hatred that I might face. This was over twenty years ago when things were considerably worse than they are now. She worried about whether I would ever be happy.

"But Miriam embraced who I was. One day after school I came home and found a package on my bed. I opened it up and found a book. *The Joy of Gay Sex*. I'm not kidding. Have you seen that book? Have you seen the *drawings* in that book? I know some of you are laughing now, but it wasn't funny to a sixteen-year-old to get a book like that from his mother. It was embarrassing. It was mortifying. But it was also deeply touching in a way I could never tell her because I could never talk about that book. I haven't told her to this day. But it was the kindest thing anyone ever did for me. I haven't the slightest doubt that you read that book from cover to cover before you gave it to me. And some of its contents must have shocked you. In fact, I wouldn't doubt if there was a long moment when you considered *not* giving it to me. But you did.

"I still have that book, Mom. You didn't know that, did you? There are pages falling out. I won't tell you which ones.

"In the next two or three years my mother helped me come out to the rest of the family. She told my father. She told my sisters. And I was lucky, none of them blinked an eye. If anybody had wanted to bully me, all I would have had to do was send my sisters after them. That's a scary sight, believe me.

"To be honest, I think Mom got way more excited about me being gay than I was. She jumped into the cause with both feet. It was Miriam who marched in the Pride parade every year with the other mothers. Some of you saw that TV news interview she did, right? I was so embarrassed after, I couldn't show my face in a bar on Church Street without someone wanting to buy me a round. And then when AIDS came down on us my mother didn't look away. She visited my friends, she fundraised for Casey House, she organized a protest against a fundamentalist speaker who had been invited to the university by a religious group. I remember what she said back then. You have to stand up and call an asshole an asshole. Always eloquent, my mother.

"It turned out that she was just getting warmed up. Because now came the fight over changing the law. When did that start? Five, six years ago. Full equality for gay partners, including the right to marry. You'd almost think that my mother went to law school, the way she started talking. And I'll tell you honestly, I had my doubts. In fact, we argued, didn't we, Mom? I called marriage a bourgeois institution. A capitalist tool in disguise. A historic instrument of female oppression. You get the picture.

"Sure, my mother said. But why shouldn't gay people get the same tax benefits, have the same right to spousal health care benefits, adoption, be the natural heirs of one another's estates? I remember she looked right in my eyes. Besides, she said, there's something about marriage that rises above all of that. That can be truly beautiful. And then she said, I know you, Michael. This Miguel looks like a keeper. One day you'll want to get married.

"Don't hold your breath, I replied.

"Sure, it seems pretty funny, all of us gathered here, but I meant it at the time. And low and behold, with the work of many gay and straight people, same-sex marriage became legal in Ontario. My mother made me come to a celebration party. But I told her, this doesn't mean I'm going to get married someday. And then the feds passed Bill C-38. And she made me come to another celebration party.

"If there's one thing my mother likes, it's to be proven right. And here we are. But I don't mind. Because as of today I'm a married man. As of today Miguel Ramirez is my husband. And my mother was right. It is beautiful."

§

They brought in an electric keyboard, a guitar and a small drum kit. The chairs were moved into a ring circling the garden. Michael and Miguel had the first dance.

They'd chosen a waltz. Miriam knew that Michael hadn't wanted to dance at all but that Miguel had insisted. They placed their arms on waists and shoulders, Miguel several inches taller and no longer so slim, and moved around the garden to whistles and catcalls. Twice around and then Michael called for others to come up. Couples began to dance.

From across the garden, Zev looked at her. He turned over his hand, offering it to her, asking whether she would dance with him. And at that moment she wanted to. For Michael, she supposed, and for all the years they had been together, and even because she wanted to feel his hand in hers, didn't want never to dance again. He must have read something in her eyes because he skirted around the other couples to come up beside her.

"Dance with me, Mir. Please."

"All right." She felt his palm press against her back and now they were moving among the others. He didn't speak but held her lightly, and her cheek was pressed against his shoulder and she smelled his familiar after-shave and felt his warmth.

They went round the garden twice and then she abruptly pulled away, unable to continue. Zev stepped backwards, bumping into another dancer. Past him she saw Michael coming towards them.

"Sorry, Dad, I was just going to ask if I could cut in."

"I defer to the man of the hour," said Zev, half bowing.

Michael took her hand and she was dancing with her son, moving with her over the grass.

She said, "Thank you, Michael. For the speech."

"The thanks are for you, Mom."

"Remember when you had to go to that dance party in grade six and you were so worried? We practised to records in the living room."

"I still made Carla Schneider dizzy when we slow danced."

"I remember her. She had a crush on you."

"At least you don't have to wonder anymore why it wasn't reciprocal."

"Funny guy. You look happy."

"I am. You were right. About the magic, I mean."

"I don't care if I was right. Well, only a little."

The song ended and the tempo picked up. Miriam handed him off to one of his women friends. Men danced with men, women with women, old with young. Hannah grabbed Ivy's hand and dragged her in and they whirled around.

The buffet opened in the dining room. Andrei was talking to Sharon and Gordon. A group of friends from the days when the kids were small had lined up together with plates. Her mother was eating from a tray on her lap, Jinette on a garden chair beside her. Miriam went over and crouched on the other side.

"I'm so sorry," her mother said.

"What are you sorry about, Mom? Everything is fine."

"I'm sorry that my husband couldn't make it. He was a very good dancer."

Miriam put her hand out and her mother clasped it with surprising strength.

"You're so right. Dad was a good dancer. He was the first man I ever danced with."

"You've always been just like him," her mother said, her voice sharp. And what did she mean by that? But yes, she was very much like him. She got Jinette a glass of champagne and then took a bit of salad for herself, although she didn't feel the slightest bit hungry. Andrei found her and they sat on the sofa in the living room.

"I just wanted to say goodbye," he said. "I have a taxi coming in a few minutes. I've said my farewells to everyone else. Michael is really beaming. This is one of the loveliest weddings I've ever been to."

"I remember yours so well. I will come next week. Thursday?"

"Thursday's fine. She'll be so glad to see you. Miriam, is there something I don't know about? You seem upset underneath it all."

She put her hand on his wrist. "You've always known me too well. Even when we were young and I was an arrogant thing, you saw right through me."

"Only sometimes."

"And you rescued me, Andrei. You did."

"Enough of that. Come walk me out."

They stood up and she took his arm. They walked to the front door and out to the sidewalk and silently waited for the cab.

§

Tiny lights placed among the roses came on. A few dancers moved slowly while others sat in the garden in the fading light. Some were having dessert seconds inside while others stood on the porch smoking.

Brian was using the car to take their mother and Jinette back to Baycrest. If she went away, he could probably come in on the weekends to see her.

Mia lay nearly asleep on the sofa. Sharon carried her upstairs to bed. Zev and a couple of other men were talking about the removal of settlers on the West Bank. She looked for Michael and Miguel, afraid they would slip out without saying goodbye. They were taking an early flight to Cuba.

She picked up a tipped champagne glass and placed it on a table.

"Professor — I mean, Miriam." Enaya had come up behind her. "Thank you so much for letting me share this beautiful time. I'll never forget it."

"It was so nice having you here. Don't forget to drop your thesis off tomorrow."

"You're too kind."

She hesitated a moment and then leaned forward to give Miriam a quick hug. She walked through the front door where Solomon was on the porch, perhaps waiting for her.

Others came to say their goodbyes. Soon only a knot of young people were left, Hannah among them. They were pleasantly arguing about what bar to go to.

"Aren't you too tired?" Miriam asked Hannah.

"I'm beyond tired, Mom. It doesn't matter at this point."

Michael and Miguel had been down the sidewalk, saying goodbye to people. They found her back on the porch.

"My God," Michael said. "I've never had to smile so much in my life."

"You loved every moment of it," Miguel said.

"Yes," he said quietly.

"The house looked so beautiful, Miriam. Everything was wonderful. My sister had a wonderful time."

They heard a crash and looked across the road to see a raccoon with her three young passing an overturned garbage bin. The door opened and Sharon and Hannah came out, followed by Zev who came up beside her.

"Is nobody going to say what a great job I did?" Sharon said.

"Adequate," Michael said.

"Barely," Hannah added.

"So where are you two staying tonight?" Zev asked. "Or is it a secret?"

"Michael just wanted to go home," Miguel said. "But I booked the Four Seasons."

"Actually, Dad," said Sharon, "you're paying for it."

"My pleasure."

"Shall we go?" Michael said. "The honeymoon suite has a hot tub."

"Nice," Hannah said.

"You aren't going to take your bikes, are you?" Miriam asked.

"I'll drive them," Zev answered, trying to catch her eye.

"That's all right, we're going in style," said Miguel. "A limo is on its way."

Sharon yawned. "I'm beat and have a need to watch some bad television before I fall asleep."

Miriam felt Michael take her hand. "Don't worry, Mom. I'll still call you."

"You better."

And then they were all quiet.

§

Hannah went off in the same dress she'd worn to the wedding only with a pair of Doc Martens on her feet, and Sharon went upstairs to see if the kids were still in bed.

Which left her and Zev on the porch. She hadn't wanted to be alone with him and didn't want to be now, but when she turned to go he grabbed her lightly by the arm.

"Mir, can't we just talk for a minute?"

She looked over the porch rail to the street. "I don't see what there is to say."

"I'll call her."

"You can say her name. She *is* a person."

"All right. Moira. I'm going to call her and say that I can't see her right now. If you want me to say forever, fine, I'll say it. But I just think if we talk things out it'll be okay. I'll call her right now." He pulled out his phone. "You can even listen."

"For what reason would I want to do that?"

He sighed and put his phone back. "All right. Then what do you want to do? Just tell me, Miriam."

She wanted him not to ask her that. She wanted him to do the right thing. She wanted not to feel like shit, not today of all days. And what did she want to do? To go to Paris and find her youth? Not likely. But she wanted to understand more, always a little more.

"I'd been thinking of going away," she said. "But you know what? This is where I want to be. Hannah has just come back. The grandkids are here. My mother. There are students who actually still want to hear from me. I've got my study, my books. If I'm going to be alone —"

"But there's no reason —"

"Don't interrupt me. Please. I said, if I'm going to be alone, I'd rather it be here. Maybe for a while or maybe forever. I don't know. How can I know, Zev? The truth is that I don't want my decisions right now to be about you. I want them to be about everything else."

"Sure," he said. "I do get that."

"But it does mean you're going to have to stay somewhere else. You can't be here. I can't figure things out if you're here."

He pressed his brow with his fingers. "Miriam, I really wish we could talk about this in the morning. I could just stay over, in another room —"

"We've got a full house. No, you need to go somewhere else. Tomorrow I'm going to get the house back in order and then I'm going to take a walk and then I'm going to get down to work. And for that I need peace. You can go wherever you like, Zev. To a friend's. To a hotel. You can stay with her, like you did two weeks ago when you said you were in Chicago."

"I was protecting you."

That mild phoniness in his voice. "Well, thanks for that, Zev. And now I'm tired, so please let's say goodnight."

He started to say something but she put her hand on his arm and he gave up. Instead, he fished his keys out of his trouser pocket, walked down the stairs, and touched the remote, making the lights flash on his BMW.

She went inside, closed the door, and leaned her back on it. She closed her eyes. Of course he wouldn't go to a hotel. He would drive across the city, over the bridge and down to Kew Beach. To the apartment house with balcony views of the lake. He would walk the three floors up (she had seen the apartment house two days ago, had gone up to read the names by the door buzzer), and let himself in. He would remove his clothes and slip into the bed of a forty-seven-year-old social worker who had already left one marriage and two engagements, and who was obviously attractive and sexual and charismatic and troubled, and who would drive Zev to despair and anger and sorrow and regret. And he would call or perhaps write to apologize for what he had done, and let her know that the relationship was over, not because he thought they might get back together but because Zev, always fair Zev, would want her to know that he had been a fool.

She did feel old.

She walked through the empty rooms, debris from the party on every table, and turned off the lights. Up the stairs to the second floor, pausing to hear the low sound of a television and Gordon's snores. She needed to go to her study again and so she took the steps up and emerged through the trap door, leaving off the light so that she was among the shadows made from the streetlight that came in through the windows.

Ivy had left her book on the chair.

She sat at the desk and from a drawer she took a new black notebook and tore off the cellophane. Pen in hand, she turned to the first blank page.

What is interesting to me is the question of whether a person can know one's earlier self or if becoming a stranger to one's own past experience is just a small, inevitable tragedy. We have memories, we think we know who we once were, but do we really? I want to see whether these notes in the James book and also the letters, what sort of person they are trying to present. Whether they can be used to know this person who sometimes seems lost to me. And whether this young self has something to say to the older one, whether she disapproves of, or cheers on, or even recognizes me.

That's what I'm really interested in. Not in being young again but in knowing better this young self. And this older one, too. By letting the two meet each other, as it were. And I'll let Henry James make the introduction in his beautiful and exasperating style. Miriam, you must meet Minnie. And now you two can have a good talk and get to the heart of things.

Underneath she wrote, "I'll probably make a fool of myself." And then she drew a line through it, leaving the words crossed out but visible.

She put down the pen. She wasn't old, that was nonsense. Tomorrow morning everyone would wake up and want breakfast. Enaya would bring her thesis. She would take her daily walk, Mozart in her earbuds. Then she would come back to her desk.

But God, she *was* tired. She longed to be in bed. Her bed now. Well, all right. She pushed in the chair and went to the stairs.

Wanting to think one more time today of her father, the softness of his voice when he spoke to her.

She went down the steps, not holding the banister.

ACKNOWLEDGMENTS

My thanks to Samantha Haywood for taking such care
in finding a good home for this novel. Michele Landsberg
generously recounted to me her own experience at the
University of Toronto, not too long after Miriam's. Deborah
Willis has been a supportive and sensitive editor. A big
thanks to Kelsey Attard, Anna Boyar, and everyone at
Freehand Books. Finally, my gratitude to Rebecca Comay
for her close readings.

CARY FAGAN is the author of six novels and three story collections for adults, as well as many award-winning books for children. His books include *A Bird's Eye* (finalist for the Rogers Trust Fiction Prize, an Amazon.ca Best Book of the Year) and the story collection *My Life Among the Apes* (longlisted for the Giller Prize, Amazon.ca Best 100 Books of 2013). Cary was born and raised in Toronto, where he lives with his family.